A GYPSY'S CHRISTMAS KISS

A SCANDAL MEETS LOVE NOVELLA CONNECTED BY A KISS 6

DAWN BROWER

MONARCHAL GLENN PRESS

For everyone that believes in the magic of the holidays and finding your one true love. Sometimes it takes years, and sometimes it's the one person you least expect it to be. Don't lose hope if you haven't found someone yet. Maybe they haven't wandered back into your life again, or maybe they have yet to cross your path.

ACKNOWLEDGMENTS

Special thanks to my editor Victoria Miller. I'm always amazed at her talent, and as an editor—I've never had better. Thanks for all the hard work you do and the help you give me to make my stories stronger. I really do appreciate it more than I could ever say. Elizabeth Evans, thank you for being my rock and always reading my roughest of rough drafts. I appreciate you more than I can ever express. Thank you, Megan Michelau for proofreading too. It means a lot to me that you take time out of your busy schedule to help me.

Tenby, Wales 1803

Cold wind blew through the small coastal town with frigid efficiency. The bitterness settled into Finley Prescott, the new Duke of Clare, and he couldn't shake it. His father's funeral still lingered in his soul. The grief had been unshakeable, and Fin wasn't entirely certain he wanted to lose the grip that held him. If he managed to let go of that feeling, then it meant his father's death hadn't left its mark. He wasn't ready for the responsibility of the dukedom. His father shouldn't be dead already.

What kind of world did he live in when a man didn't live past his fortieth year? Did that mean he wouldn't have a long life? Both his parents were gone, and Fin was completely alone in the world. He had no one to lean on and share his grief with. It was the Christmastide season, and it should be a time of joy. It never would be for him again. This time of year would always mark a change in his life he'd not been ready for. He'd turned twenty the day before, and what had been his gift? His father's death, courtesy of the brutish horse Fin had given him as an early gift. He honestly hadn't thought his father would ride the stallion. Fin meant for him to use it as a stud, but his father had been insistent about trying him out. The horse had thrown his father, and his neck broke instantly.

Fin had committed patricide—at least that's what his guilt screamed to him in regular intervals...

Oh, he knew he hadn't actually done it, but he'd been the instrument all the same. If he'd not given his father that damn horse, he'd still be alive. That kind of shame would never go away. He would have to live with that truth the rest of his miserable days. Perhaps he wouldn't die at a young age. The older he lived, the longer he'd suffer for the crime he'd committed. He deserved to suffer.

Fin walked along the shoreline, staring out at the sea. Maybe he should leave Wales for a time. It was his home, but did he really deserve to be there? They would all stare at him, either judging him, or pitying him. Either way, he didn't want to look in the faces of those around him with their mixed emotions messing him up more with each passing day. He didn't pay attention to where his feet lead him. He roamed up the hill and into the small town. There was a small shop that gypsies ran—or rather the husband of one, when the weather turned too cold for the small family to roam the lands.

He'd never gone inside, and found it odd that they had a shop at all. It wasn't normal for a gypsy to be tied down, but the shopkeeper's wife settled in Tenby during the colder months for her husband and their children. They kept their own hours and mainly remained open during the winter. The rest of the time they were gone. He had to wonder how they could make any profit with the store open for such a short time.

He headed toward it, his curiosity too much for him to ignore. Fin reached the door and tested the door knob, surprised to find that it turned. He stepped inside the shop. There didn't appear to be anyone inside of it. The shelves were nearly empty. Candles filled one of them in different sizes, ranging from long, tapered candles to thick, oblong ones. He picked one up and tested its weight. They seemed solid enough...

"Can I help you, my lord?"

Fin opened his mouth to correct her—he was a duke—as he turned. He met the gaze of one the most ethereal girls he'd ever seen and decided against chastising her—his title didn't matter. She had violet eyes and hair the color of the night sky unfettered by stars. He bet her midnight locks would be lovely dressed with diamonds, and would put a star-studded sky to shame in its beauty. She had it plaited with a long braid that fell to the middle of her back. The girl couldn't be more than fifteen or sixteen, and he shouldn't be admiring her. Maybe when she grew up... He shook that thought away.

"I don't know if anyone can help me," he finally said.

"You have a great sadness in you." Her voice held an almost ethereal quality to it, but perhaps it was just how he perceived her. He'd never met anyone quite like her before. "Please, come sit and I'll tell your fortune."

Fin didn't believe in such things, but it would help delay his return home. He didn't much feel like gathering around mourners and their sympathetic gazes. He'd made enough of a mess of things, and there was no fixing it. He might as well humor the girl and let her tell his fortune. Fin walked over to a

4

chair in front of a table. She sat on the other side. "Give me your hand."

"Does it matter which one?"

She shook her head. "No, whatever one you're comfortable with."

He lifted his left hand and set it on the table. She flipped it over and trailed her fingers over his palm. The gypsy was quiet for several moments and then she glanced up at him. There was a bit of surprise in her glance, but whatever had earned that particular look, she kept to herself.

"Tell me, my lord, do you believe in love?"

"I'm not sure I do. Nothing in my life has made that particular emotion well received." He'd experienced far too much loss. "Do you?"

She smiled. "Love isn't for everyone, and I'm young yet. I've at least witnessed the possibility."

Try as he might, he'd never be able to explain why he'd been drawn to her from the moment they met. There was something unidentifiable about her— almost special. "Do you have a name?"

"We all have names, my lord, even you."

Fin wanted to laugh at her words. He was acting rather silly and deserved that response from her. This small moment of time with her had lightened his mood quite a bit. There was a truth in her eyes that told him she'd never lie to him. He needed more people like her in his life. "If I tell you mine, will you share yours?"

"Perhaps," she replied cryptically.

She'd known he was of noble birth since the moment she'd started talking to him. He hadn't told her how far his rank rose to keep her from being even more formal. He wanted to keep that to himself longer, so he wouldn't give her anything other than his given name. For some reason, he wanted their relationship to be on more intimate grounds. "My name is Finley, but my close friends call me Fin." At least, they did—some might start calling him Clare now. He hated that idea already. Before then, he'd been the Marquess of Tenby. They should have called him by that title, but he'd insisted on Fin. He hoped the ones that mattered still called him that.

"It's nice to meet you, Fin," she said politely, but still didn't offer her name. She kept staring at his palm and nibbling on her bottom lip. She was so bloody beautiful, and she'd probably grow even more so as she matured.

"What is so fascinating in my palm?" he finally asked.

She jerked her head up and barely met his gaze. Had she seen something she hadn't liked? Had he been wrong and he *was* doomed to die young? Wouldn't that be rich? He couldn't say he was surprised at that fate. Not too many Dukes of Clare managed to live past the ripe ole' age of forty. If he had two more decades left, maybe he should start living it now.

He sighed. No, that little bit didn't surprise him one bit. "An early one?"

She shook her head. "Are you asking about your death? I'm afraid, my lord, I cannot predict that, someone you love will die—or perhaps has already passed... The lines are murky and broken, but that's not the fortune you need to be told." She trailed her finger across the lines on his palm and told him his fortune. "You have two paths—a fork in which you must choose. One path leads you to happiness but some heartache along the way."

He jerked back at her words. She tried to explain away the first part of her prediction, but he couldn't let it go. His death he could accept, but someone else he loved? That couldn't happen. Hadn't he already lost enough? He would refuse to fall in love and then he'd be safe from any further heartbreak. That would be easy enough to do. He didn't particularly want to give his heart to anyone, and he surely didn't want to live with the guilt of another's death.

"I think this fortune is over." He should perhaps ask more questions and demand she give him better answers, but he was afraid of the truth.

She held on to his hand. "Don't go. I can see you're already going down the wrong path. Please listen..."

He yanked his hand out of her grasp and fell backward in the chair. His head smacked against the floor, and she rushed to his side. She brushed back his hair and crinkled her brows together. "You have such pretty, golden hair, my lord and your eyes are the color of the sea on a hot, summer day. I'd hate to see either marked with blood and death. You already carry too much sadness."

Her accent almost made the words sound poetic or perhaps he had become delirious from hitting his head so hard. He reached up and twined his hands around her head and pulled her down toward him. When she was close enough, he closed the distance and pressed his lips to hers. They were a lovely pink, and so delectable to taste. She didn't fight him, and it was the one good thing he'd had in days.

She pushed on his chest lightly and sat back on

her haunches. "While that was lovely, it can't happen again."

"Do you believe in risks?"

She nodded. "Some risks are too great, but yes, there are times they are worth it. Why do you ask?"

"I've made too many mistakes in my life to risk my heart. I can't love anyone."

"That would be unfortunate," she said softly. "For you, more than anyone, needs love. Our lives are best left to fate. Some pain is worth living for. You can try to prevent it, but by doing so, you'll miss your greatest joy."

He wished he could take her advice, but he couldn't do as she suggested. It was clear to him, by her little fortune, happiness wasn't something he could afford to try for. The world would be better off if he remained alone. His pain wasn't meant to be thrust on the innocent.

"Are you going to at least tell me your name?" he asked as he came to his feet. Fin straightened his jacket and glanced at her. He didn't like the look of sadness that had filled her violet eyes. "Not you too." Fin was tired of the pity so many people bestowed upon him. Surely, she didn't know that he'd lost his father and grieved. He didn't want her to see him as damaged, even though, deep down, he couldn't be any more unworthy of her.

"My name doesn't matter. I'm leaving tomorrow, and I have no plans of returning. I doubt we will ever cross paths again."

"Then it won't hurt for you to share it."

He didn't know why it was so important to have her name, but he felt in his gut he should know it. They'd shared a kiss. Shouldn't they at the very least be on a first name basis? He knew they had no future together, but he wanted something to hold on to in the cold, dark nights ahead. He'd never have love, but he wanted this small thing.

"Lulia," she said quietly.

He nodded at her and smiled for the first time in days. "Lulia," he said her name softly. It was almost like a benediction for him. "Thank you."

"For what?" She tilted her head, her accent a melody he'd never tire of. "I've given you nothing but grief and set you on a path of destruction."

"That's not how I see it," he explained. "You have given me a purpose. I'll be stronger for it."

She frowned. "No," she replied defiantly. "You'll be alone. I'll never forgive myself for it. I pray that, in time, you'll realize there is a better choice to make.

There will be a time when you reach that fork, and when you do please choose love."

With those words, she spun on her heels and left him alone. He would probably never forget her. She was wrong though—he could never choose love. That would be the one thing he could never do. It would be the beginning of the end if he did.

CHAPTER 1

London, 1815

Something about the cold winter chill invigo-
rated Lulia Vasile, but then, she was not the normal
society lady. She'd grown up alongside her family
and embraced their way of life. Her mother was
Kezia Vasile Alby—a Romany princess. She'd
married Lulia's father at eighteen against her family's
wishes. When Lulia turned eighteen, she'd had to
make a choice of her own—stay with her father's
family or embrace her mother's. Her free spirit
hadn't felt right confined to the strictures of society
and decided to see what living as a Romany meant.

Not once had she regretted that choice. It had
led her down a wonderful path and to the one person
she considered her friend—Diana. Her friend had

married and was now the Countess of Northesk. At first, Lulia hadn't liked her friend's future husband, but the man had a way of worming into a person's good graces. Lulia didn't tell him that though. She liked making him miserable. Someone had to... The Earl of Northesk could be a tad arrogant at times. Lulia wanted to ensure her friend's happiness, so if it meant keeping the earl second-guessing what she might do—then, yes, she would browbeat him as often as possible. It was Lulia's way of protecting her friend, and she would do almost anything for someone she cared about.

Today Diana had planned a soiree of some sort. Lulia would much rather be fencing, or really anything other than socializing. The things she did for friends... If Diana wanted her to—Lulia shuddered—socialize, then she'd do her best. She walked up to the Earl of Northesk's townhouse and rapped her knuckles on the hard surface. When Diana had lived alone in her father's London home, Lulia had waltzed in without a care, but there were certain boundaries in place she had to follow now that Diana had wed the earl. They deserved a certain amount of respect and privacy, even if they had servants around them. Lulia would not be rude.

"Miss Vasile," the butler greeted her. "So good of

you to join us today. Lady Northesk will be pleased."

She scrunched up her nose. "Of course, she will." It didn't take much to please Diana these days... "She's as happy as a bee in a fresh flower patch. Move aside now." Lulia brushed past him and entered the foyer. All right... Some habits couldn't be broken. She hated standing on ceremony. "Where is she holding this soiree of hers?"

"You'll find all the guests in the drawing room," the butler answered. "A few have arrived thus far."

The old man had a stiffness to him that made Lulia question his humanity. No person should be that—straight. He barely moved, even when he bowed to the lords and ladies of the *ton*. It was probably a result of too much starch in his clothing. He couldn't possibly breathe well in all that taut clothing. "I'll see myself there," she told him and left him alone in the foyer. Lulia visited often enough she might as well reside there. It was for that reason that she could find her own way and didn't require an escort.

Laugher echoed through the hall. That was the only sign of life she received as she headed toward the drawing room. When she entered, she found Diana, her husband, Luther and two other people. The butler hadn't lied when he'd stated not everyone had arrived. She didn't know the other individuals. Well, that wasn't completely accurate either. She did recognize the man. He was Lord Northesk's friend, the Marquess of Holton. The lady at his side she didn't know though.

"Lulia," Diana said gleefully when she finally noticed her arrival. "I'm so glad you decided to attend." Her friend came over and hugged her.

"Was there any doubt?" Lulia stepped back from Diana's embrace and lifted a questioning brow. "You were quite insistent. So why do you need me here?" Truthfully, Lulia couldn't deny her friend much. It had been that way since they first became acquainted when Diana was fifteen. The four years separating their age made little difference. In some ways, Diana was the sister Lulia never had.

"I have some news," Diana replied. "We'll talk more later. Come meet Lord Holton and his cousin."

Diana pulled her over to the group near the center of the room. Lord Holton was a handsome man with sandy brown hair and mesmerizing hazel eyes. She could see why Lady Katherine Wilson was taken with him. At some point, those two would figure out they were meant to be together—once they got out of their own way. Diana smiled at Lord Holton and his cousin. "I'd like you to meet my dear friend Miss Lulia Vasile." Then she turned to Lulia. "This is Lord Holton and Lady Lenora St. Martin."

"It's a pleasure to meet you," Lord Holton said smoothly. He appeared the perfect gentleman, though Lulia had a feeling he disapproved of Diana's relationship with her.

"It is," Lulia agreed even though, so far, it hadn't been pleasant. "And you as well, Lady Lenora. How are you on this fine day?"

"Oh..." She glanced down. "I'm..."

The lady was a shadow of who she would eventually be. Lulia could almost see her future self. One day she'd blossom into a strong, independent woman. With Diana and Katherine's influence, she'd discover who she was meant to be. Lulia would help where she could, but she was no society matron. Her role was best left to the background. "You're lovely," Lulia supplied for her. "Perhaps you'd like to visit the refreshment table with me. I'm parched."

"Oh, I suppose I can do that." She glanced at Lord Holton and then back at Lulia. "Um... If you'll follow me..."

Lulia smiled to herself and then brazenly met Lord Holton's gaze. Let him disapprove. He'd come to realize it meant nothing to Lulia. As long as Lady Lenora didn't come to harm from her boldness, she saw nothing wrong with thwarting the marquess. She spun on her heels and followed Lady Lenora to a nearby table. A punch bowl, tea service, and tiny sandwiches were displayed artfully on top of it. Lady Lenora nibbled daintily on her bottom lip. "Do you prefer punch or tea."

Neither really... If given the choice she'd rather have a snifter of brandy. "Punch will do nicely," Lulia answered. "I can serve myself." She reached for a tiny goblet and filled it with the fruity mixture. "Do you not want any?"

"Oh, no," Lady Lenora answered. "I'm too nervous."

The little bird would take a lot to come out of the nest on her own. Lulia would work with her a little and encourage Diana and Katherine to as well. Lady Lenora was far too timid, and she'd be crushed when the season began again. How could Lord Holton have allowed her to close herself off from everything? Lucky for them both, Lulia couldn't turn away from a lost soul. Lord Holton wouldn't thank her at first, but in time he'd see why she was a blessing for Lady Lenora. "Why?" she asked. "Are you not amongst friends?"

"Yes, I am." She glanced away. One day she wouldn't be afraid to meet a person's gaze. "I'm not comfortable here. I'd rather be at home—in the library. Books are more relatable to me."

"Well, that's no way to live now, is it? Everyone needs someone at some point. Don't close yourself off to the possibility of meeting new people. You never know when you might meet the love of your life."

She shook her head. "I doubt love is in my future."

"Don't you worry about it. When you're ready for it, or even when you least expect it, love will find you."

Lulia believed in love—for other people. Lady Lenora may have already met her match but hadn't realized it yet. Sometimes, the man was the obtuse one; however, this particular lady was more oblivious than most. A gentleman could flirt with her, and she probably wouldn't notice.

"I wish I had your certainty," Lady Lenora said softly. "But I'm not brave enough to explore love. Almost everything is frightening to me."

Lulia placed her hand on Lady Lenora's arm. "Maybe not now, but one day you will." She took a sip of her punch, and then set it back down on the table. It was a terrible mixture that was bland—a bit of water would have been better than the punch.

Perhaps she should have had the tea... "Let's join the others again."

They turned to walk back to Diana and her guests, but someone else entered the drawing room. Two someones to be exact. Both had dark hair and striking features, but Lulia was drawn to one of them. He'd always be familiar to her. That man had haunted her dreams nightly, ever since their first meeting. A part of her had started to believe they would never cross paths again. She lifted her hand to her chest and reminded herself to breathe. Perhaps he wouldn't recognize her. She'd been curious about him after their initial meeting and uncovered his identity. Back then he'd been so melancholy and for good reason. A man on the brink of leaving his youth behind shouldn't face it alone, and especially without his father. It must have been difficult for him to suddenly hold the mantle of the Clare Dukedom.

"Do you know the gentlemen?" Lady Lenora asked gently. "Do you wish to stay by the refreshments longer."

"No," she answered. She wasn't sure if it was for recognizing the gentlemen or to staying by the table. Either way, the answer worked. Staying by the refreshments would perhaps encourage one of the gentlemen to come over to them, but Lulia didn't want to give the Duke of Clare a reason to speak to her. If she could avoid him, she would. "Let's take a stroll around the room instead. I find I'm restless." A truer statement had never been uttered. She'd run out of the room as fast as her legs would carry her if it wouldn't embarrass Diana.

"The one gentleman is friends with my cousin," Lady Lenora offered, but didn't indicate which man. Lulia hoped it wasn't Clare.

"Oh?" She lifted a brow. "And what does that mean to you?"

Her cheeks pinkened at Lulia's question. The lady had tender feelings for the gentleman she spoke of. So perhaps she had already found love, but love hadn't sparked between them both. "He's Holton's friend—nothing more."

The lady doth protest too much... "I don't think it's that simple. Tell me about him," Lulia encouraged. "I've been known to be a bit of a matchmaker at times. I can even tell your fortune if you'll allow me." She'd done it often enough as a young girl when she worked at fairs. It was one of the first things she'd learned living amongst the Romany. They taught her many things, but fencing was what she loved. Fortune telling had its uses—like easing Lady Lenora into trusting her, but it wasn't her strongest gift.

21

"The duke is one of the biggest rogues of the *ton*," she said. "I doubt he even sees me." Lady Lenora glanced away from Lulia and toward a nearby window. "I may as well be invisible."

So, it was Clare she spoke of... *Drat.* "Some men are blind until one day they're not. Don't discount him yet."

It had been several years since Lulia had last laid eyes on the Duke of Clare. He was as handsome as she remembered—no, more so now with age. He had a scar across his cheek that hadn't been present then. Maybe he'd received it while at war. He'd join Wellington's campaign versus Napoleon against the better advice of those around him. Sometimes Lulia believed Clare had a death wish. It had been evident in his eyes when she'd met him at fifteen, but even more so now. There was a darkness to him that remained prevalent.

"I've known him most of my life—it's who he is. I wouldn't want to change him either way. I wonder who it is he's with."

"The Duke of Clare?"

"Is that who he is?" She lifted a brow. "Imagine two dukes at one soiree. How often do you think that happens?"

Who was the other man then? She was curious

now that she realized they were not speaking of the same person. "I'm not acquainted with your duke. What is his name?" She wasn't familiar with a lot of the members of the *ton*.

"Julian Everleigh, the Duke of Ashley," Lady Lenora answered. "How are you acquainted with the Duke of Clare?"

"His ancestral estate is in Tenby," she answered. "Near where my father's family is located."

Truthfully, her father's family was a county over from Tenby. The village was where her father had decided to settle down. His family hadn't approved of his choice in wife any more than her mother's had liked her marrying him. It left them both on the outskirts of their families, and Lulia torn between two worlds. "Would you like to meet him?"

She doubted Clare remembered her. At first, she didn't want to find out, but now she had a bit of morbid curiosity about him. She wouldn't know unless she went over to him and discovered the truth for herself. Lady Lenora would give her that opportunity whether she realized it or not. She didn't wait for her to answer. Lulia looped her arm with Lady Lenora's and guided her across the room. It was time for them both to seize control of their destiny.

CHAPTER 2

Fin noticed Lulia the moment he'd stepped into the room. She was no longer a young girl. A vibrant woman had replaced her, and he found her even more attractive now than he had then. Perhaps that was a good thing. She'd been no more than sixteen at the time—four years younger than he had been. Her midnight locks were plaited into a braid that looped around her head in an elegant style. Her eyes were still a violet-blue that he found enchanting. Everything about her made him come alive—and he couldn't have her. He'd stayed away from Tenby because he'd believed, if he returned, they'd cross paths again. He should have realized he couldn't avoid her forever. Fate wanted them to be together. He fully believed that now. What a fool he'd been...

She was heading toward them with a lovely red-haired lady at her side. He still didn't understand why she was at this soiree. It was the last place he ever expected to find her. Lulia wasn't a society miss. Her gypsy roots were evident in her features. When they reached their side, he nodded at them both. Lulia met his gaze, not once glancing away.

"Hello, Your Graces," the young lady greeted them. She was a shy one and kept her gaze low.

"Lady Lenora," Ashley greeted the lady with Lulia. "It's lovely to see you out in society."

"Holton insisted," she replied. "Have you met Miss Lulia Vasile?" Lady Lenora gestured toward her.

"I have not," Ashley replied and then glanced at Fin.

He was uncertain how to answer that. They had never been formally introduced. The one time they'd met, they'd exchanged their given names. Should he admit that they'd crossed paths before? Would it ruin her reputation somehow? He mentally rolled his eyes. Lulia was a gypsy. Did she even have a reputation to protect?

Lulia took the question out of his hands. She must have sensed his indecision. She smiled at them both. "It's a pleasure to meet you both."

"I'm the Duke of Clare," he responded and felt ill-prepared for meeting either lady. "Ashley insisted I accompany him to this. Otherwise, I'd have gladly remained in my townhouse." That sounded rather dull, and didn't do him any favors.

"It would be a shame if you had." Lulia's accent was thicker than it had been in her previous statements. "You would have missed a fine soiree. Lady Northesk is a wonderful hostess."

Fin wouldn't have known one way or the other. He tended to keep to himself and didn't attend any society functions as a rule. He didn't believe he deserved anything resembling happiness. That kind of life was for other people. It was far safer and much better if he didn't impose himself on others. After the fortune Lulia had told him several years ago, he'd decided that he'd live a solitary life. He wished he'd never crossed paths with her again. If he'd known... "I'm sure Lady Northesk is lovely. I should find her and pay my respects."

He had no wish to converse with the hostess, but if it gave him some distance from Lulia he'd gladly reach for the reprieve. His stomach was a ball of knots, and he had no idea how to unravel them. Maybe once he put some space between him and Lulia, he'd feel at ease. Somehow, he doubted it would be that simple. Now that they'd found each other again, his life was bound to come unraveled.

"What a lovely idea," Lulia replied. Her warm smile startled him for a moment, and even made him feel—happy. "I'll walk with you. I've not had much time to visit with her myself. She had something she wished to discuss with me earlier."

He should have known... Lulia seemed determined to stay by his side. He didn't know why, but Fin didn't like it. She'd tried to help him all those years ago. Perhaps she felt responsible for him, but he would have to disabuse her of that notion. She didn't owe him anything, and he didn't want her to interfere with his life. He was perfectly fine with the way things were. "I..."

"Do you even know which lady the countess is?" Ashley lifted a brow. "As often as you socialize, I doubt you know anyone other than me in this room."

"That's not true," he said belligerently. There were more guests than when they'd first arrived. "I do recognize a few of the gentlemen here from our club." Though he didn't actually talk to most of them...

"Holton doesn't count," he said. "You should meet Northesk though. He doesn't come into the club as much as he used to, but he's a good friend."

"I'll be happy to introduce you," Lulia said. "Lady Northesk is a dear friend of mine."

"I had heard that," Ashley replied. His lips twitched slightly. "I must admit that I've been rather curious. Northesk has given us some interesting details about you."

"Oh?" She lifted a brow. "Such as?"

"Tell me," Ashley began. He had a wicked smile on his face as he asked, "Are you really a superior fencer?"

Her lips tilted upward slyly. "Perhaps we will have a match and you can determine for yourself."

Fin didn't like the interaction. He wanted to protest, but also realized he had no right. Lulia was not his. He had no claim to her or any reason to stop them from fencing. Though, truthfully, it was the flirting he really objected to. He turned to Lulia, and much to his surprise said, "I'd love for you to introduce me."

"Wonderful," she said, then smiled. "Let me lead the way."

She stepped toward him and looped her arm with his. They glided across the room in near silence. He, uncertain what to say to her, left it to Lulia to choose a topic of conversation. When none was forthcoming, he found himself struggling to come up with one. He craved to hear the lilt of her voice as she spoke. It had been too long since he'd heard it, and now he wanted it more than ever. She visited his dreams each night, but reality was so much better. "How have you been?" he finally asked.

"So, you are ready to admit we're acquainted now?"

"I didn't mean to imply otherwise." He frowned. "Did you wish for me to claim a prior association?"

She shook her head. "Don't concern yourself with my comfort, Your Grace. I don't bother with society much. If Diana didn't insist on having me attend her soirees, I'd gladly stay at Fortuna's and work on my fencing."

Fortuna's? He had no idea what she was talking about—other than the fencing part. Fin wanted to see how well she held herself in the sport. Perhaps he'd inquire about a match between them. He wasn't as good as he used to be, but he could hold his own. It had been a while since he bothered with the exercise. "What brings you to London?" It was the one thing he'd been dying to know.

"Diana," she said simply. "She's—family. At least more than anyone else has ever been."

Fin found that interesting. He knew her family owned the store in Tenby. Had something befallen them? It would probably be rude to ask her that outright in their current setting, but he also didn't know when he'd have the chance again. It wasn't as if they traveled in the same circles—normally. This was an oddity he couldn't explain. How had she come to consider Lady Northesk family? "How long have you been acquainted with the countess?"

"For several years now," she replied and tilted her head to the side as if in thought. "We met the summer of 1805." She smiled. "So, it's been over a decade now. I hadn't realized how long it had been."

Lulia had met Diana two years after their first encounter. He couldn't help wondering what had brought the two women together. They were as far apart in social class as two individuals could be, yet Lulia appeared to fit seamlessly into the society function. She even had a proper gown of blue and silver silk draping her lovely curves. "That must be wonderful for you to have such a close friend."

Most of Fin's friends weren't really that. They were more—acquaintances that he attached himself to from time to time to stave off the loneliness that often took root. He wanted to live a more exciting life, but fear kept him in check. Fin refused to start a life only to have it ripped away from him. He had never fully gotten over the accident that had taken his father's life. He still believed he'd be alive if Fin had never bought him that stallion. At least Lulia wasn't letting anything like fear hold her back. She was as vibrant as he remembered.

"It is nice," she agreed. "But she can't give me the time she used to. She's building a life here with Luther. I once believed him a cad unworthy of her, but the love between them was always there. I am not one to stand in the way of true love. Those two belonged together from the start. Sometimes it takes a while for people to recognize a good thing, even when it is standing directly in front of them." She stopped and glanced up at him. "Tell me, Your Grace, are you still afraid of taking a risk?"

He was, and probably always would be. "It's clear you still believe love can solve all of life's problems." He frowned. "I thought you agreed to call me Fin." He didn't like the *Your Graces* falling from her pretty pink lips. He wanted the intimacy of her using his given name.

"A long time ago a foolish girl agreed to that." She shrugged. "I always knew who you were. How could I not? The Duke of Clare was a well-known figure in Tenby, and his death rocked the town."

And he'd asked her to call him Fin because that was what his friends called him. Now he didn't have many friends, and most people referred to him by his title. Something he had feared early on. It was laughable how seamlessly he'd fallen into that title. As if he had always intended to use it and had orchestrated his father's demise. He knew he hadn't, but that didn't make it any easier. "I rather liked that foolish girl," he said softly. "She was kind to me."

"Perhaps too kind," she retorted. "You were grieving, and I wanted to make it go away. I realize now that perhaps that hadn't been a kindness. You should have had some hard truths knocked into you." Her lips pursed together in disapproval. "You've lived a lonely existence. I never wanted that for you."

"It wasn't your decision to make." He hated that she was upset with him. He didn't even know why it distressed him. Because how he lived his life shouldn't bother her at all and he couldn't fathom why it did. They weren't really friends, and she wasn't even a lady of good breeding. What she thought should never have mattered to him, yet it did. "I'm a duke. My opinion matters above most."

"And I thought I'd been the foolish one..." She shook her head and then sighed. "When was the last time you visited your home?"

He wasn't a fool. Fin knew she meant his home in Tenby. He could have played obtuse and told her he went home every day, but that wasn't the truth. He hadn't been to his ducal estate in a very long time.

"When was the last time you did?" he snapped. He didn't like where her line of questioning was heading. "I'm a grown man. I don't have to answer to anyone."

She laughed softly. "Then quit acting like a spoiled child. Quit running from your troubles."

Fin frowned. He didn't think he had been, but perhaps she was right. Maybe he should return to Tenby and lay rest to the ghosts that haunted him. He didn't want to, but sometimes a person had to face their greatest fears. It was nearing the time of year when his father had died. He hadn't been to Tenby since that Christmas. "Will you go with me?" Fin couldn't believe the question had left his mouth. Perhaps he'd imagined it.

"I thought you'd never ask..." Her smile brightened. "But I can't go yet. I have a few things to do in town first. Perhaps in a sennight?"

That was even closer to the anniversary of his father's death. He could do it. Fin reminded himself to breathe. "All right," he agreed before he could change his mind. "Send me your direction to Clare Manor. I'll have a carriage retrieve you at dawn, a sennight from today." He wasn't sure if he could handle seeing her before then. He might change his mind a thousand times before then.

"I'm looking forward to it," she answered. "Now, let me introduce you to Lady Northesk. You'll love her."

Fin wasn't so sure about that, but at least they'd changed their topic of conversation. Though he doubted that subject would leave his mind any time soon, nor would Lulia. He still couldn't believe he'd found her again... Maybe it was meant to be. Fin wouldn't dwell on any of it, or at least he'd try not to. He had a trip to plan.

CHAPTER 3

The little soiree Diana planned was more of minia-ture ball without dancing. Lulia didn't understand society's need to have so many planned entertain-ments presented to them for their pleasure. Surely they could find other amusements. But, of course, they couldn't... They were all spoiled children pretending to be something more important than they actually were.

She had so much disdain for the lords and ladies of the *ton*. They had all looked down their noses at Lulia for her entire life. She could name a few who didn't. Diana had always supported her, and those she called friends were kind to her as well. Diana's husband had started to come around, but even he hadn't thought highly of Lulia at first. In fact, the sole gentleman who seemed to like her and not view her as damaged was Fin. That should surprise her, but it didn't. Just because he was a duke didn't mean that he wasn't a good man.

Lulia had a few prejudices of her own... The difference was that she owned them and had plenty of reasons for their existence. Lulia continued across the room with Fin at her side. They hadn't said a word the entire trek toward Diana. He didn't seem to know how to carry on a conversation, and that suited Lulia for now. They'd have time later to uncover each other's deepest secrets.

"Diana," Lulia greeted her friend. "I'd like for you to meet an old friend of mine." Perhaps that was a slight exaggeration. They did have a prior acquaintance though. Diana didn't exactly need to know how brief it had been.

"Oh?" Diana lifted a brow. "I didn't realize you had any other—friends..."

Lulia held back a laugh. Diana had met all of Lulia's friends, so it didn't surprise her that she was a little shocked to realize she knew a peer other than her. At least one that Diana hadn't introduced her to. "This is the Duke of Clare," she explained. "His home is near where I grew up."

Diana scrunched her eyebrows together in

confusion. Lulia didn't often talk about her own family. There was a very good reason for that, and one day she'd explain it to her. With Lulia's mixed heritage, she had never felt as if she belonged anywhere. "It's always nice to meet someone Lulia considers a friend. What brings you to London, Your Grace?"

"I've been in London for a while. I find home a tedious place to be." Fin's answer was as cryptic as Lulia expected.

"There are a lot of individuals such as yourself, who prefer *ton* life to that of the country," Diana said. She smiled at Fin. "Lulia hasn't adapted to it as much as I'd have liked, but she's braved it for me."

"Country life is preferable," Lulia agreed. "And I'll return there soon."

"I didn't realize you had plans to," Diana said and then frowned. "Don't feel as if you need to stay in London on my account. I understand if you need a break from the demands of the city."

Lulia would have to tell Diana that she planned on returning to Tenby with Fin. She wouldn't like it, but she would understand. There were a few other things she had to finally tell her friend. She had a secret, and Lulia wasn't entirely certain how Diana would react to it. "I'll come for tea tomorrow and explain my plans. If that's all right. You don't have any more soirees planned, do you?"

Diana laughed. "I don't have anything immediate planned. There are a few things I'd like to discuss with you as well. Tea would be perfect." She nodded at Fin. "It was wonderful to meet you, Your Grace. Please come for another visit. Any friend of Lulia's is always welcome." Diana practically seeped warmth and happiness. "Now, if you'll excuse me, I see Lady Katherine. There is something I must discuss with her."

Lulia hadn't noticed Lady Katherine arrive. She was an intimate friend of Diana's, and also had always been kind to Lulia. Lady Katherine had romantic feelings for Lord Holton, but she thought no one else noticed. Lulia saw everything, and one day she'd be able to gloat about how she'd recognized the match before the two future lovers had. It was easy enough to predict where the couples would end up. For a lot of years, she didn't think she'd have love either. Now though, she was starting to believe it might be possible.

"There are a lot of people here." Fin pulled at his cravat. A thin line of sweat beaded on his forehead. She had always thought him handsome. Like a golden god too unsure of himself to take over the world. She would find a way to help him out of his protective shell. "I'm not sure how long I'll be able to stay."

"You're not in favor of a crowd." Her lips tilted upward. "I understand. They can be a bit much. If you think this is bad, you should definitely avoid a ball."

"I've always done better in smaller settings," he replied. "There is a certain intimacy that soothes me. This..." He gestured toward the people in the room. "Is maddening. How do people find a way to have a decent conversation in a crush like this?"

Lulia shrugged. "I wouldn't know, Your Grace. I don't converse with anyone at these things—other than Diana and a few other individuals. I don't have the patience for the rest of them." After meeting her father's family she'd taken on a distinct dislike for high society. Technically, she had the breeding to rub elbows with all the nobs, but she didn't want to. They were all too snooty for her.

"I'm afraid I must leave." He pulled at his cravat again. "This has been lovely, but..."

"Say no more," she replied and then smiled at him. "I understand. We'll see each other again. Next time in more pleasant surroundings."

Fin nodded and then spun on his heels to exit the

room. Lulia let him go because they would see each other again. They had a future to figure out. He hadn't realized it yet.

LULIA HADN'T STAYED at the soiree long after Fin had left. She didn't like them much, and Diana had been too busy playing hostess to spend much time with her. So, Lulia had said her farewells and then left. Now, the afternoon after she found herself once again on the Northesk doorstep. She lifted her hand and rapped on the door. The butler opened it and nodded at her. "Miss Vasile, please come in. Lady Northesk is waiting for you in her sitting room."

Lulia really hoped Diana actually had tea and sandwiches or even cakes. Her stomach rumbled as she walked down the hall. She hadn't eaten anything, and her lack of food had caught up to her yet. Luckily, the sitting room was at the front of the townhouse, so she didn't have far to go. She entered the room and found Diana perched on a chair with an open book on her lap.

"Good afternoon," Lulia said as she headed toward her. She took a seat on the settee. "How are you on this fine day?"

"I couldn't be more wonderful." Diana lifted her lips into a smile. "I'm glad you've finally arrived, and before you ask..." She held up her hand, silencing Lulia. "Tea will be here shortly with plenty to eat. I know how you are when you don't have any food. Cook is sending in a full spread."

"Now, that is fantastic news," Lulia said. "I am a bit hungry."

"You always are." Diana shook her head.

Complain once about the food being served late... Lulia sometimes wished her friend would let that go. ... "I am not." She scrunched up her nose in displeasure.

"Do you want to tell me about your friend the duke?"

Lulia would rather not. There were things she didn't quite understand about Fin yet. Much to happen before they were in a place where she could say anything with certainty. "There's nothing to tell. He was a neighbor, and we crossed paths occasionally." Could one encounter be considered several? It had certainly seemed like it. That one meeting had been seared into her soul afterward.

Diana lifted a brow. "There's a story there, and I fully expect all the details. Don't hold back now Lulia. You never have in the past."

That's where she was wrong. She had kept a lot from Diana. When Lulia had decided to keep parts of her life hidden she'd believed it was for a good reason. She didn't know how Diana would react to the truth. Her friend could have turned out to be a society miss who would look down on those of a lower class; however, she had instead embraced everything about Lulia. Diana had come off as snobbish at their first meeting and invoked her father's name to ensure Lulia continued the conversation. Not long after that though Lulia had realized she was a sweet girl in desperate need of guidance. The real Diana had shown through then. "I'm capable of keeping many secrets," Lulia said softly.

A maid pushed in a tea cart and poured cup for each of them. The food would probably come in later, but Lulia was grateful for the tea. It gave her something to do with her hands and to concentrate on. She put two sugar cubes in her tea and stirred.

Diana sipped her tea and then focused her attention on Lulia. "I'm sure you are capable of keeping several secrets." She set her tea cup on a nearby table. "That became clear to me last night when you introduced me to a duke. Was he a beau of yours?"

Lulia had been mid-sip when that question slipped out, and she nearly spit tea all over herself.

That would have been a disaster... She set the teacup down so she didn't accidently spill it too. "Of course not," she said. "He's an acquaintance, nothing more." Though she'd like him to be something else entirely —one day. Maybe even soon... He hadn't given her the opportunity to fully explain his fortune all those years ago. She would like a chance to rectify that and perhaps put him on a less dark path. "A friend who needs my help, much like you have in the past."

That long ago fair, when they'd first met, Diana had wanted to learn how to fence after watching Lulia acting out a scene from *Romeo and Juliet*—the fight scene. It never would have occurred to Lulia to offer to teach her the sport, but it had given her a reason to become acquainted with her.

"He wants to learn fencing?" Diana's lips curled into a keen smirk. "That has to be a way for him to..." She wiggled her eyebrows. "...spend quality time with you." She chuckled lightly. "I would think the Duke of Clare would have access to the best fencing masters available. Don't let him convince you to tutor him in a skill when he wants something more—*decadent* from you."

Lulia rolled her eyes. "He's not in need of lessons of any kind. It's something more...delicate than that." Fin needed a friend to accompany him to Tenby and face the demons of his past. Lulia didn't want to tell Diana that. It wasn't her secret to share.

"Is he in search of a lover then?" Diana frowned. "I didn't think he'd be that...blunt. Don't sell yourself short. You deserve better than to become some duke's mistress."

"He doesn't want to offer me anything of the sort." Lulia sighed—though she wasn't averse to becoming his lover. Lulia never believed she'd actually marry anyone, but she would like to know the more intimate side of marriage. She'd be willing to bet he'd be rather good at making love too. She'd have to tell Diana everything or she'd never let it go. "I promise he is a friend. When I was sixteen, I told him his fortune and it's haunted him—I need to help him see past it. For that, he needs to go home, and I do as well."

Diana nodded. "I see. So you're going to travel with a duke to...?" She scowled. "It occurs to me that I don't know where you consider home to be. I am not acquainted with the duke to ascertain that information myself. Where is his seat located?"

"Tenby, Wales," Lulia answered matter-of-factly. "And before you start to besmirch his reputation and mine—there's nothing untoward happening." She leaned forward. "Now, can you forget about the duke for a moment? I have something much more important to discuss with you. I should have told you years ago, but as time went by, it became harder and harder to tell you the truth."

"You can tell me anything. Surely you know that..." Diana reached over and placed her hand on Lulia's. "You're my dearest friend. There isn't anything you could say that I'd find troubling."

"That is because you haven't heard it yet." Lulia blew out a breath. "I hope, after I'm done, you can find it in your heart to forgive me."

"You're scaring me..." She pressed her lips together into a fine line.

Lulia hated this part. After the words left her mouth, there would be no taking them back. Their friendship would be forever altered, and Diana would never look at her the same again. "My father wasn't a gypsy and my surname isn't Vasile." She stared down at her tea. "At least not completely. It's Lulia Vasile Alby. My father is Lord Geoffrey Alby, the third son of the Earl of Chaucerton."

"But..." Diana's mouth fell open. After several heartbeats went by, she finally found her voice and said, "My mother was the daughter of the Earl of Chaucerton. That would make your father, my uncle, and you..."

"Your cousin, yes," Lulia replied softly. "We're family."

This was the moment Lulia had feared for years now, and the reason she'd agreed to participate in that county fair all those years ago. She'd wanted to become acquainted with her female relation. A cousin she hoped would embrace the relationship. But once she met Diana, she couldn't tell her the truth. She had wanted a tutor, not a cousin, and Lulia had embraced the opportunity to be a part of Diana's life. Lulia hoped that she wouldn't push her away now that she knew the truth...

CHAPTER 4

The silence in the room was nearly deafening as she waited for Diana to respond fully to the information Lulia had imparted. She swallowed hard and sat back against the settee. The rattle of wheels against the floorboards echoed down the hallway. Lulia stared at the closed door of the sitting room fully expecting it to swing open at any moment. Her assumption proved to be right when it did, and then one of the house maids pushed the aforementioned cart inside. The tray was filled with tea cakes and tiny sandwiches. Normally, Lulia would be already on her feet and preparing a plate. Now though, she feared any food would upset the nervous rumbling of her stomach. The maid pushed the cart until it was next to the tea service, then turned to Diana and asked, "Will there be anything else, my lady?"

"No, Beatrice," Diana answered and then gestured toward the door. "Please see that we're not disturbed, and the door remains closed."

Beatrice nodded and left the room, shutting the door behind her. Diana sat forward and met Lulia's gaze. "Why didn't you tell me sooner?"

Lulia wished she had a good answer to give her. She should have confessed sooner. It would have made everything so much easier if she had owned up to her real reason for being a part of the county fair so many years ago. By the time that fair had come around, she'd been living with her mother's family for two years and discovered it really wasn't the life she wanted. She had some of the Romany inside of her, but at her core, what she really needed was family. Being on the outside of both worlds, she never believed she'd find a place where she belonged. Her father had kept no secrets from her. Lulia had always known about her relations on both sides. Neither one had ever truly accepted her, so it was no surprise she didn't believe that Diana would either. "My parents died when I was eighteen," Lulia began. "I was given a choice. I could live with my mother's family or my father's, but not both. Neither my paternal grandfather nor my maternal one wanted me though. It wasn't an easy choice to make, but I believed at the time I'd feel more at home with my mother's family." She'd been wrong, and it hadn't taken her long to discover that truth; however, once she'd made her decision, she couldn't take it back. Her paternal grandfather had told her never to darken his doorstep again. "They were closer to the ideal I was used to. My father humored my mother, and we lived off the land during the warmer months, and in the winter we retreated to his shop in Tenby."

Diana tapped her fingers on the arm of her chair. Her lips were pursed, and she narrowed her eyes into slits. "That doesn't explain why you've lied to me all these years." Lulia's stomach rolled as anxiety spread throughout her entire body. She hated that Diana might be upset with her.

"I haven't lied," Lulia said. "Merely withheld all the information." She tucked a stray lock of her hair behind her ear. "Please be patient and let me tell my story."

"Then by all means finish it." Diana waved her hand. "I've nowhere else I need to be."

She was surprised Diana had been this accommodating thus far. Lulia probably wouldn't be if their positions were reversed. "Grandfather Alby won't acknowledge me as his granddaughter. Once I picked the Romany, he disinherited me. He told me if I contacted anyone in the Alby family he'd ensure that I'd regret it." She took a deep breath. "I believed him."

"And yet you've been a part of my life for nine years now." Diana shook her head. "What changed?"

"I found out recently that grandfather passed." Diana had doubts. Lulia didn't blame her for having them either. "He didn't know I've been in contact with you. When is the last time you've visited him? I don't recall you ever making the effort."

She sighed. "You have me there. I didn't particularly enjoy spending time with any of my grandparents, but our shared one was especially difficult. I've barely corresponded with him, and only when necessary. He didn't even attend my wedding."

Lulia was aware... If he had come to town for Diana's wedding, then it would have meant she couldn't attend herself. "So, you see how it was easy enough to keep my secret, but I couldn't do it anymore. Even if I hadn't received notice of his death... I needed you to know the truth."

"Honestly," Diana began. "I had wondered why a gypsy would abandon her family and choose to stay in London with me. It never made sense." She crinkled her nose. "When did grandfather pass? I haven't received word. Are you sure he's gone?"

"It's recent. Within the past fortnight. One of the Romany who still travels in the area wrote to me about it. I don't think she'd lie to me." She sighed. "I'm half Romany," Lulia explained. "I don't mind putting down roots, but I still have a more primitive side. I like my freedom—I've enjoyed controlling my own life. You've given me that option by supporting my endeavors over the years."

"This is going to take me a while to become accustomed to." Diana moved forward and placed her hand on Lulia's shoulder. "I would never have believed we're family, but I admit it is a welcome revelation. I've always felt some sort of kinship toward you."

Lulia smiled. "I'm glad you have considered me family from the very beginning. You've always made me feel—wanted. If not for you I don't know where I may have ended up. Thank you for being such a wonderful person. You've been a true inspiration to me."

A tear fell down Diana's cheek. She wiped it away as quickly as it appeared. "Don't make me cry. I'm overly emotional these days."

"Why? What's wrong?" Lulia's heart started to

pound at her words. Diana was the only family she had. Well, the family that mattered...

"That was my news I wanted to share with you." Diana's lips tilted upward into a serene smile. "If you hadn't shocked me with yours, I'd have already imparted it—I'm with child."

"Oh..." Lulia's already racing heart nearly burst with the announcement. "That's splendid."

Her stomach rumbled, and Diana laughed. "You have to eat something. Cook made sure to make your favorites."

Lulia's cheeks pinkened. "It's embarrassing sometimes how hungry I get."

After that, any tension that remained in the room dissolved into nothing. The rest of their visit went unencumbered, and they eased back into the comforts of their longstanding relationship. Everything had gone amazingly well and much better than Lulia could ever have hoped for. She shouldn't be surprised. Diana had a generous heart and had always accepted her. It might take her a while to recognize Lulia as family, but she could be patient while Diana worked through it all. Now she needed to make things right for and with Fin.

FIN STARED at the correspondence on his desk and the words blurred. He hadn't been able to stop thinking about Lulia and the soiree from the previous day. She'd always been there at the back of his mind. That fortune she'd told him so many years ago. Everyone in Tenby had known about the gypsy that resided in town, but he'd never thought to seek her out. Lulia was her daughter. Did she really have the power to see the future? Could he believe that his fate depended on what path he decided to take, and was it too late to choose the right one?

How was he supposed to get any of the accounts done if he couldn't concentrate on them? His mind was a bloody mess of contradictions. He had to get out of the house and try to forget about what bothered him. A walk might work wonders in clearing his head—or a ride. He hadn't exercised his horse in a while. This time of year, Rotten Row would be nearly empty. The lords and ladies of the *ton* didn't appreciate the cold.

"Halsey," he hollered.

Thump, thump, thump echoed through the hallway and into his study. His butler had been injured in the war, and his badly damaged leg gave him a permanent limp. He'd been Fin's aide while he served in the Cavalry. If not for Halsey, Fin might have died. Fin had a long, jagged scar across his shoulder where a blade had sliced through him. It would have hit his heart if Halsey hadn't knocked the enemy soldier to the side, changing his trajectory.

Halsey limped into the room, leaning heavily on his cane. "You bellowed, Your Grace."

"Don't be impertinent," Fin said, but couldn't stop his lips from twitching. Halsey kept him honest and grounded. "Have someone bring my horse around. I am going out for a while."

Halsey left the room at a slow pace. It would give Fin the time he needed to prepare for a gallop in the frigid temperature. He closed his account ledger and put his quill back into the ink pot. When he returned, he'd finish the task. For now, he'd take the time to embrace life and decide what he wanted. The desire he had for Lulia was as much a part of him as breathing. He didn't want to disrespect her. Just because her mother was a gypsy didn't mean Lulia would welcome the idea of becoming his lover. Fin would take great pleasure in making love to her, and he wanted Lulia more than anything. He wasn't sure how to approach the topic with her.

He buttoned up his winter coat and then pulled on his gloves. Not long after that Halsey's hard footsteps filled the hallway leading to the foyer. He stopped at the edge of the stairs and met Fin's gaze. "Your horse awaits you outside."

"Good," Fin said. "I don't know how long I'll be. Have Cook hold dinner. I may go to the club."

He had never sought the advice of his peers. Most of the time he believed himself impervious to society's dictates, but the few acquaintances he'd managed to acquire from his brief induction to White's might prove useful. The Duke of Ashley was a known reprobate and seducer of women. He stayed clear of innocents though. Something told Fin that Lulia, for all her worldly airs, was as innocent as any young debutante on the brink of their debut. Still, Ashley might have some insight Fin could use to charm her. Ashley attended White's more than he went home—so the club would be as good a destination as any.

Halsey nodded. "Very well, Your Grace. Should I inform Brixton that you'll not need his services too?"

Fin frowned. He wasn't sure if he'd go that far. His valet might still be needed, but Halsey might be right. "Yes," he replied. "I'll see to my own needs tonight. Tell him to attend to me in the morning."

With those words, he left Halsey in the foyer. The butler understood his duties and would ensure everything in Fin's household was taken care of. His servants were well trained and knew their place. Fin hopped down the steps and took several long strides toward his stallion. He mounted the horse and took the reins from the footman. "Thank you," Fin said and then pressed his knee into the horse to bring it to a canter. He was pleased to see he had been correct that the streets were not busy due to the cold.

He debated taking his horse to Rotten Row or heading to the club first. After a moment of internal deliberation, he motioned his mount to head toward the park. Once he arrived there, he let the horse loose into a fast gallop. The rush of wind over his face was invigorating, and he'd never felt more alive than in that moment. Perhaps Lulia had been right and he hadn't truly been living. He was rather disappointed with everything as a whole. Fin had never wanted to live such a mundane lie. At first, he'd done so out of a sort of necessity. After his horrible fortune he hadn't wanted to invite anyone he might come to care for into his life. Then, as time went by, it had become more of a habit than anything else. Now he might have to rethink how he had chosen to live. He brought the horse to a walk and headed down the path toward town. Now that he'd gotten the exercise he needed, Fin would go to White's and see if Ashley was in attendance.

When he reached the club he dismounted and tied his stallion to a nearby post. One of the club's grooms would take him to the stable while Fin attended. He took a deep breath and entered—Fin had never been more nervous in his life.

Hopefully it was worth the effort and Ashley could help him gain the one thing he'd always desired—Lulia...

CHAPTER 5

Fin went to the back of the club where there were several tables set up for card games. Ashley sat at the one in the far corner. He was flanked by the Marquess of Dashville and the Earl of Darcy. The duke shuffled cards in front of him. They couldn't really be about to play a game yet. They were a player short... Maybe he could take advantage of the empty chair and try his hand at a game. Truthfully, he didn't really care to play, but it gave him something to do while he prevailed upon Ashley for a bit of advice.

"Gentleman," Fin greeted them. "Care if I join you?"

"Have a seat," Darcy gestured toward the empty chair. "How do you feel about a bit of whist?"

He doubted he would be much good to his partner, but he wouldn't explain that much. He'd pay Ashley's marker if they ended up losing. "I don't mind the game." Fin shrugged. "Let's play."

Dashville picked up his glass and downed the contents. "Hey," he shouted to a nearby servant. "Can you bring me a decanter of brandy?"

"Right away, my lord." The man said and rushed off to do Dashville's bidding.

"Have you read that latest scandal sheet?" Ashley said. "That Lady X sure knows how to rake a man over the coals."

Fin scrunched his eyebrows together. "Lady X?" He didn't read anything other than *The Times* and had no idea what scandal sheet Ashley meant.

"Grrrr..." Dashville groaned. "Don't get me started on that evil woman. She has written about me five times this month." He held up his hand and waved two fingers at them. "Twice in the last edition! None of it was good either. She hates me. I'd bet everything I own on it. What did I ever do to her?"

The servant came back and set the decanter of brandy on the table. "Will there be anything else, my lord?"

"Bring His Grace a glass," Darcy motioned toward Fin. "He needs to catch up. We've been drinking..." He turned to Dashville. "How long has it been now?"

"Damn if I know..." Dashville poured some more Brandy into his glass, then turned to Ashley. "Are you going to deal?"

Fin felt as if he was in a whirlwind. The conversation was beyond him and he didn't want any brandy. He didn't need an addled brain while he played cards. Especially since his card skills were lacking. "I don't need a glass," he told the waiter. "We have everything we require for now."

"Very well, Your Grace," the servant replied and then left.

Ashley shook his head and met Fin's gaze. "You don't always need to be so bloody proper." He started dealing the cards. "There is such a thing as pleasure. I suggest you find something of that nature."

Fin's lips twitched into a smile. "I've never been good at letting my guard down." He could sometimes be a bit impulsive, but he didn't have any real vices.

Dashville lifted his glass and saluted him. "I wish I could say the same, and maybe that awful woman would quit writing about me."

"Let it go," Darcy said to the marquess. "Lady X will tire of writing about you at some point or maybe quit giving her the tantalizing gossip she needs to put you in her column."

Dashville glared at the earl. "That's easy for you to say. She hardly ever mentions you unless it's in conjunction with me." He was really concerned about this Lady X person. Perhaps Fin should figure out what all the fuss was about.

Dashville and Darcy were close friends. As long as Fin had been aware, the two lords had always been by each other's side. Their easy banter said a great deal about how comfortable they were with each other. Fin wished he could have that easy of a relationship with another person. "Considering how often you're in my company, that's a bloody lot." Darcy grinned. "You're lucky I like you or I'd have had to let our friendship go. She really doesn't favor you."

Ashley leaned back in his chair and had a large grin on his face. For whatever reason he seemed to be enjoying Dashville and Darcy's conversation... The cards he'd dealt remained face down on the table. The earl and the marquess showed no signs of picking them up. Fin left his where Ashley had laid them too. He didn't see any reason to pick them up until the other men decided to play.

"You would be lost without me," Dashville said.

He picked up his cards. "I thought we were playing... What game is this again?"

A laugh spilled out of Fin's mouth before he could prevent it. He'd been worried about playing horribly when Dashville didn't even recall the game they'd decided upon. "How inebriated are you?"

"Not nearly enough," the marquess replied. "As I'm sure you may have deduced, I've had a rotten couple of days."

There was a time when Fin had been tempted to drown his sorrows in brandy, but he didn't think he deserved the numbness alcohol would offer. The only way to get over the pain of losing his father was to go through it. In the end, it made him stronger and maybe a little wiser. Though even he still made foolish mistakes... "Does this have to do with the mysterious Lady X?"

"Don't get him started on that particular subject," Darcy warned. "He won't stop discussing the evil workings of her mind as it is."

"That's all he's mentioned since I sat down at the table." He met Dashville's gaze. "What did she write in her column?"

"That's not the correct question to ask, Your Grace." Dashville picked up his brandy and took a long drink.

Ashley shook his head. "Are we going to play this game or not?"

"You never said what game you dealt us for," Darcy said. "Dash forgot."

"I thought we were playing whist," Fin supplied. "Am I wrong?"

He might not know a lot, but he did understand how to pay attention when need be. When he came to White's, he'd hoped for some advice on how to court Lulia. Now though, he realized he might as well give up on that particular endeavor. Darcy and Dashville were too foxed to be any good, and Ashley seemed weirdly preoccupied. Fin would still stay and play cards though. It would do him some good to do something resembling a good time. He hardly ever let go and enjoyed himself.

"You're not wrong," Ashley answered. "This is definitely whist."

Darcy picked up his cards and glanced at them. "Then let's get this game going."

Fin took this as his queue to do the same. He slid the cards toward them and then adjusted them in his hand. Once he had the cards the way he wanted, he waited until it was his turn to lay a card down. The other gentlemen remained silent for several plays. It was odd considering how vocal they'd been up until that point. The game moved at a rapid pace, and before Fin had time to realize it, he had no cards left in his hand.

"That was the fastest round of whist I've ever played," Ashley said aloud. "Did any of you actually think about what you were doing, or did you randomly throw a card on to the table?"

Dashville shrugged. "I couldn't say."

Ashley quirked a brow. "You can't say? Are you bloody serious?"

He shrugged. "I think my mind went blank for a spell. I can't be held accountable for my actions. I think I may have had too much brandy."

Darcy's low throated chuckle was the only answer Dashville received to that statement. Fin could have told the marquess he'd had too much to drink when he'd walked into the room. Someone should confiscate his brandy decanter before he poured himself another glass. "I don't usually play at all, so I couldn't say how fast it should have gone." Though he did think it was a rather quick game. "I'm not sure..." He met Ashley's gaze. "Did we win?"

"I'm sitting at a table of imbeciles." He threw his hands up in frustration. "Not sure why I'm bothering anymore."

Fin sighed. "If it makes you feel better, I didn't

come to play cards at all. I was hoping to gather a bit of advice from you."

"Oh?" Darcy sat up a little at that. "I'm a bit intrigued. What does the proper duke need assistance with?"

"Bugger off," Ashley told him. "He wanted my advice, not yours."

They were going to start another round of bickering if Fin didn't do something to prevent it. Was it too much to ask for some simple conversation? Maybe he should call it a loss and go home. Coming to the club hadn't gone at all as he'd imagined.

"Maybe this was a horrible idea," Fin said. He pushed the cards in front of him to the center of the table. "I'm going to leave."

"Don't go," Dashville said. "As you can tell." He gestured toward them all. "We're falling apart at the seams. We don't exactly have our lives—together. But if you're willing to take what we have to say..." He nodded at Ashley and Darcy. "We'd be happy to impart on you some tidbits we've learned the hard way. What is it you need help with?"

"There's a woman..."

Ashley leaned forward. "You have my full attention. Is it Miss Vasile?"

Fin's mouth fell open. How could he have

possibly known that he was taken with Lulia? "Pardon me?"

"Don't act so shocked. I read people well, and you, my friend, were clearly taken with Lady Northesk's gypsy friend."

"That's not how I'd describe her."

He considered Lulia the most beautiful woman he'd ever seen. She had haunted his dreams for years now. Fin had been attracted to her from the first moment he'd met her. Of course, no one sitting with him knew that. They were barely acquainted with each other, and Fin had just started to become familiar with Ashley. He'd thought he needed friends, and he still did. Living his life as he had been —it was a lonely existence.

"That doesn't matter." Ashley waved his hand dismissively. "What does is the fact that you are smitten with her. What is the problem?"

"I don't know how to..."

"Seduce a woman?" Darcy supplied. "If that's the case, you did come to the right place." He smacked Dashville on the shoulder. "According to the scandal sheets, he's the biggest rogue of us all."

"Hell," Dashville nearly grumbled the word. "It's one scandal sheet. Stop bringing that blasted woman up."

"So, none of you know who this Lady X is?" Fin was starting to be glad he'd never graced the pages of her scandal sheet. Though he wasn't sure if that was true or not as he'd never actually read it.

"That woman doesn't matter," Dashville said. "She's not your problem. We can help you with yours. Tell us about your gypsy."

He had come in for advice on how to pursue Lulia. Was it selfish to brush aside their concerns about Lady X for what he needed? He did want to have a real relationship with her. This might be his one chance to figure out what to do next. "She's beautiful."

"Of course she is. Any woman worth the effort is." Darcy wiggled his eyebrows. "But what makes her special?"

Fin sat back in his chair and considered his question. What was it about Lulia that kept his attention focused on her? "She's brave, stubborn, and intelligent. When I'm around her, I can't focus on anything else. Even when she drives me mad, I want her by my side. Her tenacity and willingness to put those she loves first is amazing. I can't imagine a more perfect woman than her."

"Sounds like love," Ashley said. "A lot of good men are falling victim to it. First Northesk, and now you." He sighed. "I suppose we'll have to help."

Fin wasn't sure what he felt for Lulia. The idea of love terrified him and he wasn't sure he wanted to define his feelings yet. Loving her might prove fatal and he didn't like the idea of losing her. All he wanted was to enjoy spending time in her company. Whatever was between them could be determined later.

"Helena's Christmastide ball," Darcy said. "I'll have my sister, Helena, send out the invite. It's the event to be at if you're still in town. If you're both there, it'll give you some time to sneak away if you want to."

"Your sister won't mind?"

Darcy shrugged. "It's mother's idea, but she doesn't like organizing these things. Diana won't care." He stood. "I'll take care of it now. I might need to find my bed regardless."

Fin wasn't sure how a Christmas ball was the answer to his problems, but he was all for spending more time with Lulia. At least when they were around each other he had a better chance of figuring her out... "I think I'll depart as well." Fin pushed back from the table. "I'll see you all at the ball?"

Dashville lifted a brow. "Probably. Helena hates

me almost as much as that dratted Lady X. She'll invite me though because she loves her brother."

"I'll be there," Ashley said, ignoring Dashville's rant. "To offer you support. Go home and rest. I'll stop by tomorrow, and we can discuss everything."

He didn't have a plan exactly, but he did have something. It was a start any way... Perhaps after he had a lengthy conversation with Ashley, he'd have a better idea how to court Lulia. Fin could use all the help he could get...

CHAPTER 6

Lulia had not heard from Fin in several days. She hadn't heard from Diana either. She debated what to do about both of them. Should she go and visit Diana, or should she let her cousin come to her. She understood that it was a lot to take in and that Diana may need time to come to terms with the new parameters of their relationship. At least Lulia had plenty of time to accept that they were family. If Diana needed space to figure things out on her own, then she would allow her to have it.

Fin was an entirely different story. They have had years of separation and barely were acquainted with each other. If they had any chance of discovering who they were as individuals and as a couple, they would need to find time to enjoy each other's company. The problem was that Lulia had no idea what Fin wanted. Hell, at times she had no indication what she hoped to gain from their association. Did she want a lover, a friend, or did she want something inherently more than that?

A part of her envied Diana and her relationship with Lord Northesk. They loved each other with a passion Lulia didn't quite comprehend. She believed her own parents had adored each other, and they'd risked so much to be together, but she'd never experienced anything similar to that type of devotion. What would it be like to be loved and have that love in return? Could she have that with Fin?

Fin may not know where she resided; however, that did not mean she had no way of contacting him. Luckily, for her, the Duke of Clare's residence was well-known. There was a simple solution to her problem. She would write a missive and have it delivered to the Clare townhouse. When she sent her note, she'd leave her direction, as he'd requested from her, and then it would be up to Fin to take the next step. She wanted the opportunity to discover if they had anything worth fighting for. Lulia needed to find out if she was capable of loving a man.

She didn't doubt she could care for another person because she adored her cousin Diana. Fin was an entirely different beast though. The very idea of him was almost foreign to her. When she was sixteen his presence held the promise of a future she never dreamed of or thought she could have. Her mixed heritage made finding a husband difficult at best but nearly impossible at worst. She resigned herself to a life of living alone. It was for that reason she sought out her cousin Diana to begin with.

Once she decided to send Fin a missive, she walked over to her desk and pulled out a parchment. She dipped her quill into a pot of ink and then began to pen her note. Once completed, she sealed it with wax and went to find a servant to have it delivered. Her roots were more humble, but working with Diana over the years, she'd amassed a nice savings. It allowed her to keep a simple residence with a couple of servants. She had a cook who, at times, took on the role of housekeeper as well. It was her footman she gave the note to for delivery to the Clare townhouse.

"Please ensure this arrives safely," Lulia said to Maxwell. "It's important that the Duke of Clare receives it."

"You may depend upon it, Miss Vasile," Maxwell replied. With those words, he spun on his heels and exited her home.

She had no idea what she was going to do while

she awaited his reply. What if he didn't answer her? Should she take things a step further if that should happen? How far could she theoretically push him before she received the desired response? She wanted him to express how his feelings, to believe in the possibility of something more, to want love, and her. He seemed to want more from her in the same way she did with him, so she had to believe her efforts wouldn't be for naught. Lulia hoped she didn't have to discern his feelings on her own. She'd prefer he freely admitted them to her.

Maybe she should go visit Diana. Her cousin wouldn't push her out of her life entirely. Lulia would not allow it. She had worked so hard to build a relationship with Diana and she refused to give up on her now. The rest of her family had pretty much abandoned her. Diana was the only one she had left, and now that she was expecting a child of her own, Lulia had even more to lose. Lulia wanted to be a part of Diana's life, as well as the lives of any children she may have. She refused to be pushed aside and forgotten again.

It was a day of decisions. Lulia had made one by sending a note to the Clare townhouse. Now she had to make another one. Should she go to visit her cousin or allow Diana the time she probably needed?

Everything inside of her screamed to run as fast as possible to see Diana... Lulia understood the dilemma that faced her cousin. She'd been in her position once. Maybe it would be better to send her a note as well to gauge her reaction in that manner. When Maxwell returned, she could send him out to deliver it too. With that in mind, she went back to her desk and quickly wrote to Diana.

Before she had time to seal the note with wax a knock echoed through the room. Someone was at her door, but for the life of her, she couldn't figure out who it could be. There were not many individuals who had her address. She could name them on one hand, and most wouldn't bother to visit. With Maxwell out attending to Lulia's errand, it was up to her to answer.

Lulia headed to the front of the house and pulled the door open. A servant stood on her doorstep with a note in hand. It couldn't have been from Fin because Maxwell had left moments before. Maybe it was from Diana, but she doubted it. Mainly because she didn't recognize this particular servant. "How may I help you?"

"I have an invitation for a Miss Vasile," the man explained.

"You do?" Lulia lifted up a brow. Who would've

sent her an invitation? "You may give it to me." The man handed her the wax-sealed envelope. She nodded at him and then closed the door. She tore off the seal and scanned the invitation. After reading it, she was more confused than ever. Why would the Duke and Duchess of Montford have sent her an invitation to their Christmastide ball?

FIN WAS ONCE AGAIN STUDYING the ledgers for the accounting on his estate. The numbers swam before his eyes as they had before, and every other time he bothered to try to take care of the ducal estate. He had no business even attempting to work. His focus was on other things. To be more accurate, every aspect of his thought process revolved around Lulia. He should give up while he was ahead. Though he couldn't really be certain he was actually ahead of anything. The accounting could be off, and he really should start at the beginning when things were clearer.

Fin scrubbed his hands over his face and tried to wipe away the thoughts of Lulia. Although he didn't know why he bothered... Nothing would remove her from his thoughts. Resigned to his current state of mind, Fin stood and walked over to a nearby cabinet. He opened the door and pulled out a decanter of brandy. Normally, he didn't have much room in his life for stronger spirits. After his time at the club playing cards, he had found a new appreciation for the numbing effects alcohol provided. He hadn't had any to drink that night, but since then, he had found a way to keep his cabinet supplied of the amber liquid. He still hadn't received his invitation to the Duke of Montford's ball. He didn't doubt that the Earl of Darcy had ensured his sister would send him an invitation. Darcy had no reason to lie to him.

He poured two fingers of brandy into a glass and returned the decanter to the cabinet. His time would be better served preparing for the upcoming ball. He should pay a visit to his tailor and have a new waist-coat, tail-coat, and pantaloons fashioned. Fin didn't usually care much about his style of dress. He had an excellent pair of Hessians since he had already taken measures to replace his old pair of top-boots, but he hadn't bothered with a new wardrobe at all. Now he found he had a reason to present himself in the best light.

Fin stared down at the brandy he poured. He twirled the goblet between his fingers and stared at the liquid as it coated the sides of the glass. While he appreciated the brandy's ability to numb everything, and yes, his mind and body, he wasn't sure it was so wise to depend on it as much as he had for the past couple hours. A knock on the office door echoed through the room. Fin didn't really want to deal with anyone; however, he did have a duty to the dukedom to see to. Therefore, that was why he bellowed out, "Come in."

The door creaked open as his butler entered. The old man was hunched over and used a cane to help him limp to Fin's side. When he reached Fin, he handed him two missives. "These came for you, Your Grace."

Fin took the letters from the butler. "Was there anything else?"

"No, Your Grace," the butler replied.

He nodded at his butler and then dismissed him with a wave of his hand. "Please see that I'm not disturbed."

"Very well, Your Grace." The butler slowly turned to balance himself on his cane for support and hobbled out of the study. As he exited, the butler closed the door behind him with a soft *click* echoing back at Fin.

It was a rare occasion that Fin received any missives outside of the occasional note from his solicitor or the steward at his estate in Tenby, so to have delivered two at the same time baffled him. As to the writer of the other letter, he could only guess. Although it would be easy enough to deduce who had written him by unsealing both of them. Fin slid his finger over the wax seal on one of the missives. This one he recognized—it was the crest of the Duke of Montford. He picked up a letter opener and broke the wax off. It was indeed what he expected it to be. A Christmastide ball would take place on the first of the twelve days before Christmas day to launch the season. He had less than a day to prepare. If he wanted new attire for the ball, he'd have to pay an extravagant sum to have it commissioned. Some things were worth the effort though.

He set the invitation to the ball aside, then returned his attention to the second one. This wax seal was not one he was familiar with. He wasn't even sure it resembled a crest of any kind. It looked like two fencing swords crisscrossed with a rose between the two hilts. Fin broke the seal and began to scan the contents. His lips turned upward into a joyous smile once he realized who the note originated from. His Lulia had grown impatient.

. . .

My darling Fin,

I grow weary awaiting a response from you. Patience is not one of my finer attributes, and I find it easier to reach out and take what I want. Please meet me at Vauxhall Gardens tomorrow directly following afternoon tea.

You will find me where the roses bloom under the hot summer sun. Let us pray their beauty survived under the exquisiteness of a winter storm. I'll be awaiting your arrival on bated breath. My thoughts will be of you until we meet next.

Yours always,

Lulia Vasile

He applauded her ingenuity and anticipated their time together at Vauxhall Gardens. Though he would have to investigate the area to solve the riddle... She wanted to play a game, and who was he deny her anything? The gardens would be nearly empty at this time of the year, and it would be the perfect place to steal the kiss he'd been longing for. Then maybe, just maybe, they could be something more to each other.

CHAPTER 7

Vauxhall Gardens was a landscape public garden
with an orchard, long walks, arbors, and hedges. The
site also boasted streamlined promenades, gravel
paths, fountains, artificial ruins, illuminated trans-
parencies, statues, platforms for musicians with thou-
sands of lanterns to light the entire garden. There
wasn't much Vauxhall didn't have to offer to both
high society and the lower classes. Its popularity
reigned during April through June. In those months,
it became a particular pleasure point for the upper
class. It cost three shillings to enter Vauxhall, and
once there, visitors could marvel at the many thou-
sands of gas lamps illuminating the gardens. They
could be found hanging in festoons from the trees
and between the cast iron pillars of the vaulted

colonnade. At one time, the only way a person could gain entrance was by taking a boat over the Thames; however, it was more easily assessible now by way of the Westminster Bridge.

Lulia had always been fond of Vauxhall Gardens. Even during the cold months when the gardens weren't in full bloom. They were perhaps more appealing to her during those times when the snow covered the statutes, the fountains, and the pathways through the gardens. There was no revelry, no entertainments, and no lovers hidden amongst path. All of those things could be magical with the right person, but Lulia had never had anyone to share with. The snow glistened over the hedges like pieces of white magic giving the feel of a winter kingdom designed for her pleasure. Since not many people could be bothered with dealing with the hardships snow and ice brought them while visiting the gardens, Lulia found a sense of peace amongst the stark beauty of it all. That was why she invited Fin to meet her, so she could share why she loved it so much with him.

She couldn't be certain if he understood the riddle she had left for him. Perhaps she should have been more forthright and told him exactly where to go. Lulia couldn't help testing him though because she needed for him to fight for her in some small way. If he could figure out where to find her in the largess of Vauxhall Gardens, then surely he must really want to spend time with her, and maybe she meant something to him. There was nothing Lulia wanted more than for him to want her—to love her.

Lulia crossed the Westminster Bridge and headed toward Vauxhall Gardens. She paid her entry fee and strolled through the gates, then onto the path that would lead to her destination. During the summer months the garden was filled with a kaleidoscope of colors—from green, to red, to purple, to blue—a sea of every vegetation and flowers imaginable... She loved roaming through those paths, dreaming of romantic starry nights, warm breezes, and magical kisses. She wasn't too proud to admit that in most of her wildest imaginations and daydreaming Fin had taken a prominent role as a suitor of her choice. He'd made quite the impression on her and her wayward youth. And truth be told, she never truly believed she'd see him again.

She told him that he would find her whether roses bloomed under the hot summer sun. There were many places that roses grew inside Vauxhall. But there was one place that they thrived during the hottest days. Not many realized that the gardens had originated as a house known as Vauke's Hall, built during the reign of King John—hence the name Vauxhall. When it had been re-fashioned into the elaborate public garden, open to the public, some of the old estate had been left intact. There was a pavilion on the south end of the garden that during the summer had vines weaving up the side and a trellis with roses dripping down its vines. Of course, it was during the summer, in high heat, and now Vauxhall was nothing more than sparkling ice and brilliant snow. If a person didn't know the rich history of Vauxhall, they might not deduce the simple riddle she'd written.

Lulia rounded the corner and stopped short when the pavilion came into view. Standing in the center, staring at that trellis where the roses normally blended in to, stood the man who haunted her dreams—the Duke of Clare. She should never have doubted that he would comprehend what she meant. Clearly, Fin was a man who understood the importance of history. There were many gentlemen amongst the *ton* that shirked the idea of learning, both from the mistakes of others, and their own. She had hoped Fin wasn't one of their ilk. It warmed her heart to realize he might truly be her one true love. Not just because he had understood her missive, but also because he understood her.

There were not a lot of people who saw beneath the layers she pulled over herself. Lulia had a hard time allowing people to become close to her, and there was really only one individual she let in. That person was her cousin, Diana. Now, as she stared at Fin standing alone in the pavilion, she started to believe he too could be part of her inner circle.

Lulia closed the distance between her and Fin. She nearly ran up the small set of stairs and launched herself into his arms. He held her close, and his warmth spread over. She'd been hugged several times in her life, but for some reason this experience was more profound than any she'd ever had. She wanted to burn this memory in her mind forever, so that she could bring it out on the dark and dreary days when everything seemed hopeless. No one ever lived a perfect life, and all they could hope for were days that almost seemed as if they were ideal. In this one moment, with Fins arms wrapped around her, and her head lying against his chest, Lulia could not have found a more flawless instance to hold onto.

Fin had been waiting for Lulia for several minutes. He hadn't known for sure what her note referenced about Vauxhall Gardens, so he'd come early and talked to some of the gardeners and workers for more information. He learned a lot about Vauxhall. A part of him couldn't help wondering if the members of the *ton* realized that their pleasure garden used to be a vaulted estate. Maybe someday someone would write it down for the world to know. He wasn't talented with words, and therefore it would never be him, but he did appreciate learning about the history of people and places he often frequented.

Once he ascertained the location he was to meet, Lulia, he had headed there immediately. He'd known he would have to wait for her because he'd discovered the location earlier than they were supposed to meet. Fin didn't mind though. It was enough that she'd be by his side soon. What he never expected was for her to run into his arms and let him hold her. It was the most amazing thing he ever experienced. As much as he enjoyed embracing her, he had to let her go. Her warmth enveloped him and made him believe in the possibility of a future—as long as she was by his side. She ignited something in him he couldn't quite define, but he did know he liked it. Maybe a little too much... Fin released her and took a step back. "I feel as if I've been waiting forever for you."

The corner of Lulia's lips tilted upward. "Surely you haven't been here that long." Her cheeks were rosy from the cold wind, and her violet eyes were brighter because of the reflection of the sparkling snow. Even her midnight tresses seem more brilliant against the stark white of their surroundings. Fin had always found her beautiful, but now she was nothing less than breathtaking.

"It matters not how long I've been traipsing through Vauxhall Gardens. Having you here with me is the only thing I could possibly want. Now that you're here, how shall we spend our afternoon together?" Fin brushed a stray lock of her dark hair behind her ear. He was starting to believe Vauxhall Gardens had a magical quality to it. Though it was probably more likely being with Lulia left the impression on him. "Do you wish to stay in the gardens, or would you prefer go someplace warmer?"

"I adore Vauxhall," Lulia stated. "But I can see

how its charms are lost under a blanket of snow. If the cold is too much for you, I'd be happy to go wherever you suggest as long as we are together."

Truth be told, Fin had no idea where they could go. Outside of his own home, he didn't go many places in London. Unless he had an invitation to a particular ball or soirée, he remained behind the confines of Clare House. He'd recently joined White's club and started to become acquainted with more—high ranking *ton* members. He didn't want Lulia to be cold, but he was at a loss on how to prevent that and had no idea where to suggest they go.

Fin glanced down the path that would lead them to the exit of Vauxhall, and then he turned his attention back to Lulia. He lifted a brow and stated, "I don't mind the cold; somehow, it seems inconsequential as long as you are by my side. Perhaps it would help if we stroll down the pathways to keep ourselves warm."

"An excellent suggestion," Lulia agreed. "How acquainted are you with the landscape of the gardens?"

"I suppose it's time to make a small confession," Fin began. "Up until earlier today, I've never entered Vauxhall Gardens. Although, now, in order to solve your little riddle, I couldn't be more acquainted if I tried."

Lulia's throaty laughter echoed on the wind. She tilted her head back as her bemusement rolled out and made her even more enticing. Fin had not believed that could even be possible. Being in her presence and the glory of everything she allowed the world to see, Fin realized how big a fool he'd been walking away from her all those years ago. Yes, he'd been a frightened lad of barely twenty, and her no more than sixteen, but if he'd been brave enough, they could've had all those years they lost together. "I adore you," Lulia told him. "Of course you would take my riddle as a challenge and not only embrace it, but unravel it to its very core."

"Anything worth doing should always be done right," Fin stated plainly. He shrugged his shoulders nonchalantly. "You may not believe this, but you've always meant the world to me. At a time when I didn't believe there was even the smallest chance of hope, you showed me gentle kindness and stubborn determination was all I could ever possibly need to survive in this harsh world. I realize that, after that day, I ran as fast as I possibly could from Tenby and you," Fin said softly. His voice took on a husky tone as he spoke again, "But I've never been able to forget you, and as long as I live I never will. It was the fortune you told me that terrified me the most. What if I choose wrong; what if I'm already too late?"

"It's never too late to make the right decision," Lulia explained. She reached up and cupped his cheek in the palm of her hand. "Sometimes it takes a while to figure out what should be done. Maybe you weren't meant to decide what path to take all those years ago. This could be your time—our chance to be together."

"Do you remember the fortune you told me?" Fin asked.

Lulia nodded. "I'm not likely to forget." She reached for his hand and peeled off the glove. Lulia traced her fingers over the lines on his palm and recited the fortune she told him all those years ago. "You have two paths—a fork in which you must choose. One path leads you to happiness but some heartache along the way."

"And the other?" He asked as he did before.

"It means death." Lulia muttered quietly. "I didn't explain your fortune completely all those years ago and I'm afraid you misinterpreted it. Have you avoided love because you were afraid the one you loved would die?"

"I may have. I couldn't handle someone I loved dying..." He nodded his head almost absentmindedly. "I've had a lot of heartache over the years," Fin said more to himself than to her. "Maybe I unwittingly already chose my path."

Lulia handed him his glove so he could place it back over his already cold fingers. She glanced away from him and remained quiet for several moments. Then she met his gaze and said, "I'm afraid this is where you have to make a decision. Back then, you didn't make the choice. You avoided making one. Yes, there has been lots of heartache; however, that's not what the fortune meant. Loss is part of life, but the path you choose won't be about the deaths you've endured, but the love you accept. For without love, you are not truly living, and that is the path of death."

Fin recalled she had once asked him if he believed in love. At the time, it had been a resounding no. It was amazing how much clarity a man could gain in years filled with loneliness, and Fin had managed to achieve maximum lucidity in that intervening time. He didn't want to live a life of death. It would be far better to discover exactly what love was with her. Without examining his motivations to closely, Fin closed the distance between them. Then, before either one of them had time to think about it, he pressed his lips to hers and kissed her. It was something he should have done when she first arrived. Maybe, even farther back than that...

CHAPTER 8

After that magical afternoon, Lulia couldn't stop feeling as if she were floating instead of using her own two feet to carry her from place to place. When Fin had kissed her, she let herself enjoy it instead of analyzing every aspect of it. A part of her had wanted his kiss, but she'd never imagined there would be a day she'd experience the reality of his lips pressed to hers. They were making progress in their hastened courtship—if that is what they were doing. She didn't quite know yet what Fin hoped to gain by their interactions, and if she were honest with herself, at times she didn't either. It would be easy to say she wanted it all, but what did that entail? Did she want marriage? Children? Would it be easier to give in to the passion until it died down to nothing but embers on the brink of losing their heat? Didn't all romances suffer a fate similar to that?

Lulia sighed and headed into Madame Debroux's modiste shop—above the secret ladies' gaming hell, Fortuna's Parlor, where she helped run the fencing part of the club. She was visiting Madame Debroux for a different reason though. She had commissioned a ball gown for the Christmastide ball. Lulia didn't often bother with fine dresses, but she'd wanted to have something pretty for the night —for Fin. She rapped on the back door and waited for the modiste to come out. After a few moments, she peeked around the door and met Lulia's gaze. "*Ma chère*," Madame Debroux greeted her. "I've been waiting for you. Please come back so we can finalize your fitting."

She followed the modiste to the back room. Several seamstresses were already there, prepared to pin and tuck where needed. Lulia had a few gowns and didn't see any reason to have more than that made. Young debutantes or high society matrons had an excess of dresses and Lulia would never be one of them. She wasn't anything more than a half-gypsy with nobility connections. No one paid her any attention, and that usually suited her. Now though, she wished to make a lasting impression. It was interesting what a woman would do for a male she felt affection for.

"Here it is," Madame Debroux announced as she held up her creation. It was blue silk draped with silver chiffon. The bodice was crushed sapphire velvet with tiny gray beads worked in, creating an intricate design through the fabric. The skirt bellowed out more than a ball gown usually did. "I love it," she said a little breathlessly.

"Of course you do. I designed it," Madame Debroux announced. "Now we will act as your lady's maid and assist you donning it. A few alterations may be needed before the ball tonight."

First, she had to remove her current dress. Once it was off, Lulia stepped into the beautiful ball gown, and the seamstresses laced her into it. The fit was far better than Madame Debroux implied. She couldn't tell where any alterations needed to be made. It hugged her curves and displayed her bosom nicely. Fin wouldn't be able to look away from her, and yes, her décolletage. Lulia had never bothered with fineries of any sort, but in this gown, she felt like a princess about to search for her prince. She wasn't anything near royalty, and Fin wasn't a prince; however, a duke was close enough.

"It's perfect," she muttered a little breathlessly.

"Not quite," the modiste hummed through the pins she placed in her mouth. She pulled one out and placed it along the hemline. She kept going until she had every one in place and ready for the seamstresses to alter the gown. "It needs a little tucking here, and then it'll be flawless."

"Thank you so much for creating this." Lulia rubbed her hands over the velvet and sighed. "I would never have believed I'd find a dress so..."

"Quixotic?" one of the seamstresses supplied the word for Lulia.

"Yes," she answered. Everything had been turned upside down in her world. She was falling in love, or perhaps she'd always loved Fin and hadn't realized it. Either way, it seemed to be new, and Lulia reveled in that happiness. She had hope that her and Fin would find a way to achieve the life they wanted together.

"The pins are all in place," the modiste announced. "Now we must remove the dress so it can be completed. I'll have it sent to your home after the final stitches are in place."

Lulia wanted to hug her and express her gratitude, but the modiste wouldn't appreciate it. She might greet her as *my dear*, but that didn't mean she wanted any familiarity. It's who Madame Debroux was, and Lulia had accepted it a long time ago. The modiste did care for her and all the ladies involved in Fortuna's Parlor, but she didn't show affection. Her idea of caring was creating beautiful gowns for those she loved. Lulia hadn't taken advantage of that offer until now, and Madame Debroux had fashioned Lulia a breathtaking gown. She had put all her heart into its creation, and Lulia couldn't be happier.

The seamstresses untied her laces and helped her out of the gown, then carried it away to put the finishing touches on it. They didn't say a word as they left and focused on the task at hand. Lulia slipped back into her simple pale yellow day dress and then turned her attention to Madame Debroux. "I can't thank you enough..."

"Child," she interrupted her. "You never ask for anything and give too much of yourself. This is nothing in comparison. It's about time you started taking care of yourself." She winked. "Now tell me about your beau."

The corner of Lulia's lips tilted upward into a sly smile. "You mean you don't know everything?"

Madame Debroux's shop filtered gossip through it with regularity. There wasn't much that the modiste hadn't heard or could find out if she so desired. Lady Narissa, the Duchess of Blackmore, had used that to her advantage from time to time while running Fortuna's parlor. It was in the midst of having a dress created by Madame Debroux that she had decided to open the club. Lulia had joined in her endeavor when Lady Diana became acquainted with the duchess. Now it seemed as if they'd been a part of Fortuna's Parlor, and in conjunction, Madame Debroux's forever.

"I may have overheard a few things." She scrunched up her nose. "But you know how gossip is. You never can tell what the truth is or isn't unless you verify it from the source."

She was correct, of course. Sometimes gossip created a horrible scandal intentionally. The truth could be skewed as it made its rounds through the *ton*. She hadn't been a victim of gossip, but she had been witness to the harmful effects of it. There was a scandal sheet that continued to grow in popularity, written by Lady X. Lulia didn't know how the mysterious queen of secrets came by her information; however, from what she could ascertain, all of it had been true, or at least it appeared to be. The truth could be misleading out of context. One day she'd like to meet the woman behind that scandal sheet and ask her why she wrote it as well as how she came by her information.

The gossip column intrigued her. Lulia tilted her head to the side and closed her eyes. She imagined Fin and what their night might entail later. They would have a lovely evening—she wouldn't have it any other way. She took a deep breath and considered how to answer Madame Debroux's question. "Fin is...impulsive and broody at the same time. He makes decisions without considering the consequences, and is concerned about the present, but he loves deeply and is loyal to those he cares for. He carries his emotions around for the world to see, but only if you look closely enough. His gruff exterior is a shield to keep everyone at bay."

"And you love him," Madame Debroux said softly. "Do you think he'll ask for your hand? Will you too one day be a duchess?"

Lulia had no answer to that. "The future is uncertain. I'm not sure Fin even knows what he will do. As I mentioned—he's impulsive. I don't want him to do something in the moment and come to regret it later. I'm not a good match for him."

The modiste was quiet for a moment, and then she pulled Lulia into her arms. It surprised her how affectionate she was being when she too had a gruff exterior. Slowly, Lulia lifted her arms and embraced her friend. She didn't know what she'd said to make the modiste believe she needed the hug, but she was grateful all the same. "You're more than worthy of him," Madame Debroux said with a fierce tone. "Don't ever doubt yourself. He would be lucky to have you as his duchess."

Not many people knew about her father, and that she was born of noble blood. She kept that side of her life a secret. Sometimes she didn't know why she did, but it had seemed like the right thing to do. She already carried the stigma of her gypsy roots. What would they think of her if they realized she was the granddaughter of an earl? A lord who couldn't be bothered to acknowledge her existence? Her parents had loved each other. Lulia witnessed their affection and had reveled in it. Their bond had made her want to find something similar one day. Could she have found that with Fin? Did they have a chance of building something real in a world who would always consider her inferior?

"I'm glad you believe so," Lulia whispered. "But you know it won't be that simple. The *ton* never forgets."

"This is true." The modiste let go and stepped back. "They won't let you forget either; however, you want to know why that won't matter?"

"Why?" Lulia found herself asking, and for the

first time, hoping she could have it all. "What difference would anything make?"

"You'll be his duchess," she said, then her lips tilted upward into a smug smile. "They'll envy you your position in society. There's not many ranks higher than that. You can make a difference, and maybe in time, that stigma will become something of the past. I'm not going to lie to you." She placed a hand on Lulia's arm. "It won't be easy, and some days the heartbreak will be so severe you'll want to give up. In the end, you won't though. Because you'll know the truth. That you have something more precious than any of them will ever understand —love."

Lulia smiled then. The modiste was right. If she could find that with Fin, all of the fighting and disapproving glances would be worth the struggle. They could make things work for themselves and the *ton* could be damned. She wanted to have him and the life she hadn't allowed herself to imagine. That didn't mean he'd ask for her hand in marriage, but at least she understood what she wanted if he did. If he offered for her one day, she'd answer with a resounding yes. "Well," she replied slowly. "If he is suddenly struck with a need to propose marriage, and I agree to the betrothal, I'll be sure to inform you of the welcome news."

"He will," she said with an assurance Lulia didn't share. "Maybe not tonight, but one day. When it happens, I'll be there to make your wedding gown and watch you say your vows."

"If that day comes..." She smiled and let herself dream of that special day. Her lips tilted upward, and she let the happiness roll through her. "There's nothing I'd like more than for you to do all of that." Lulia hugged her quickly. "Now, I must go. I have a ball to prepare for."

With those final words, Lulia spun on her heals and walked out of the shop. She had a few more stops to make before she returned home... The ball couldn't arrive soon enough for her. She wanted to see Fin again.

CHAPTER 9

After her fitting with Madame Debroux, Lulia went up to Fortuna's Parlor to check in with Narissa. She didn't want any unexpected surprises interrupting her attendance of the ball. Narissa had already left the club and returned home, and probably wouldn't return. So, Lulia decided to go to the backroom and do inventory on her fencing gear. She didn't have anyone lined up for lessons until after Christmastide, but she liked to keep track of her equipment. The club wouldn't open for several hours yet, and no one should be around. Especially since Narissa had left. She pushed open the door to the fencing area and frowned. "What are you doing here?"

Lady Katherine stood in the middle of the room, staring at the wall. Her dark hair was tied back in an elegant chignon and her day dress was damp at the hem. The sapphire blue of the dress matched her eyes. She didn't have a smile on her face and in fact, seemed rather sad. Lulia crossed the room and stopped in front of her. "Lady Katherine." She reached for her hand and repeated her question, "What are you doing here? Are you all right?"

She shook her head and remained silent for several moments. "My grandmother..."

"What about her?" Lulia and Lady Katherine were not particularly close. The reason they had a relationship at all was because of Diana. They were friendly at least... "Is she all right?" She had a bad feeling that whatever Lady Katherine said next would not be good.

"No," Lady Katherine answered and then tears started to flow over her cheeks. She wiped them away furiously. "She's gone—forever."

Lulia was having some of the best days of her life, and here Lady Katherine had nothing but grief to greet her each morning. "I'm so sorry."

"I'm sorry for..." She gestured toward herself and then the room as a whole. "I know you didn't come in here and expect to find me. The club is the one place I can find peace and when there isn't fencing going on this is the best place to hide and think."

"Do you not have someone you can talk to about this?" Lulia didn't want to be rude. She didn't know how to handle Lady Katherine's grief.

"I'll be fine. It shouldn't have taken me by surprise, but it did." She wiped her cheeks again. "No one understood me the way she did. It'll take me a little while to accept that she's gone."

Lulia was starting to regret her decision to come up to Fortuna's. She'd never felt so out of place. She'd lost her parent's years ago and had to grow up faster than she'd have liked. Her grandparents were not the type to coddle her either. They'd done their best to make her life more difficult, whether they'd intended to or not. "There are no words in existence that will take your pain away. I wish there was something profound I could offer to help you through your sorrow, but there isn't. All I can say is that she'll always be with you—in here." She patted her chest. "Those memories you have of her will be a blessing to you one day. Hold on to them and appreciate them when they visit you later."

"You're right. I know you are." Lady Katherine lifted her lips into a wobbly smile. "I'll leave you to your task." With those words, she turned to leave.

"Wait," Lulia said. "I'll walk out with you." She wanted to ensure she arrived home safely. She could take care of her chores at the club another day. "I need to leave regardless. Tonight, is the Montford ball, and I have an invitation to attend for once. It's time I returned home and began the preparations needed to appear as if I'm a normal member of the *ton*."

Lady Katherine laughed. "I don't think you'll have to work too hard to establish that. Most of the lords and ladies won't question your presence as often as you're found in Diana's company."

She wasn't wrong, but that didn't make her right either. They tolerated her, but none of them had ever accepted her. Still, Lulia fully intended to go to the ball and ignore the contemptuous glares. They exited the club and walked down the stairs to the back entrance. Lulia didn't want to disturb any of Madame Debroux's customers. Lulia stayed with Lady Katherine until they reached the Gladstone Townhouse. Once she was safely inside, Lulia changed direction to return to her own home.

She arrived at her little cottage on the edge of London, she started preparations for the ball. For the first time in her life she decided to take her time and pamper herself. She didn't believe in it and usually was more practical, but she felt almost as if she were a princess preparing to meet her one true love. The gown had been delivered while she walked Lady Katherine home. Lulia asked Mrs. Allen to stay later to assist her into it. She usually purchased dresses that didn't require a lady's maid, but the gown that Madame Debroux designed was not one she could don by herself. The laces on the back wouldn't allow it.

She trailed her fingers over the fabric, still amazed she had such a beautiful dress to wear. It was unlikely that she'd ever wear it again, but she didn't care. Lulia couldn't wait to see Fin's expression when he noticed her wearing it. A part of her felt silly that she wanted his approval, but she couldn't help it.

Mrs. Allen came into the room. "Are you ready to dress for the ball?"

"I am," Lulia answered. She held up the dress and then stepped into it, then turned to allow Mrs. Allen to tie the laces.

"Are you going to need assistance with your hair as well?"

Lulia hadn't considered that. She usually kept her hair plaited and didn't do anything elaborate to it. "Are you talented with hair?"

"Probably not as much as an actual lady's maid is, but I can do a little."

"All right, then," Lulia said. "I suppose it wouldn't hurt."

After the laces were tied, she sat down in a nearby chair. Mrs. Allen loosened the braid and let her midnight tresses fall in waves down her back. She brushed them until there were no knots, and then began to slowly twist and pin them in place. A few stray tendrils were left loose to drape over her shoulders and frame her face. "There," Mrs. Allen said with a pleased tone. "You're as pretty as a princess. Too bad we don't have anything sparkly to adorn your beautiful hair with."

Lulia didn't even have any jewelry to wear. "I'm sure your handiwork is gorgeous enough." She slid her kid slippers on and then came to her feet. Lulia exited her room with Mrs. Allen trailing after her, and then went down to her small foyer and donned her wrap. "It's time I started walking to the ball."

Mrs. Allen frowned. "But isn't Lady Northesk going to retrieve you in her carriage?"

Lulia hadn't spoken to Diana since she confessed to their relationship. She had no reason to believe she'd go out of her way to retrieve her. "Do you know something I don't?"

"She sent word earlier," Mrs. Allen answered. "Did Maxwell not tell you?"

"No." Lulia hadn't seen Maxwell all day. She'd had a lot going on. "Did she indicate when she'd be here?" A knock echoed through the room, immediately following her question. "That must be her now."

Mrs. Allen opened the door and a footman stood on the other side. "Pardon me," he said respectfully. "Is Lulia Vasile Alby in residence?"

He'd used her full name—even the part she'd stopped using years ago. That must be Diana's way of telling her she fully accepted Lulia as her family. She would probably even go so far as to make her announce herself thusly at the ball. It would cement her place in society—it was her birthright, after all. Lulia shook her head and stepped around Mrs. Allen. "Is Lady Northesk here to retrieve me now?"

"Yes," he replied. "If you'll follow me."

Lulia exited her home and shut the door behind her. Mrs. Allen would ensure the house was closed up properly before she retired for the evening. The footman led her to a nearby carriage and assisted her inside. Diana and Luther sat on one side, and she took the seat across from them.

"You look lovely," Diana said. Her face lit up with a happy smile. "Are you ready to announce to the *ton* that you're my family?"

"As ready as I'll ever be," she said softly. She hoped that Fin would find the news welcome. "But I never needed society to know about our connection. It's enough for me that you do."

Diana reached for her hand. "I know. But I don't want to deny our relationship. You've always meant a lot to me, and while it was a surprise—I'm happy to call you family. Let me have this."

"It's best not to argue with her," Luther said. He had a wicked grin on his face. "She usually gets her way."

Lulia chuckled softly. "You're right. She does— have it your way. We'll announce it formally at the ball."

"Good," Diana said, a little too pleased with herself.

Lulia settled back into the seat and did her best to become as comfortable as possible. She might not have anything resembling comfort at the ball once the *ton* realized her connection to Diana. Lulia was the legitimate grandchild of an earl. That made her Lady Lulia Vasile Alby, and not the mere miss they had all believed.

FIN HATED BALLS. Yes, He had wanted to attend this one so he could dance with Lulia, hold her in his arms, and pretend, for a while, that they had a chance at forever. He adored her and wanted to believe they had a future together. After he was announced he headed to the card room. He couldn't be sure how long it would take for Lulia to arrive, but he didn't want to remain in the ballroom long without her nearby. The matrons of the *ton* would consider him available to thrust their daughters upon him if he did.

There were a few eligible duke's remaining in society, and he, unfortunately, was one of them. That made him one of the most desirable bachelors. Ashley, being a duke, was equally desirable, followed quickly by the Earl of Darcy as an heir to a dukedom. The only other person the mamas hoped would choose their young debutantes was the Marquess of Dashville. All of them were supposed to be in attendance of the Montford Christmastide ball, making it the most attended non-season function.

"The Earl and Countess of Northesk," a servant announced. Fin turned to look toward the entrance. Lulia could be arriving with them, or maybe he was hoping she would. "Lady Lulia Vasile Alby," the servant bellowed out her name. Fin froze in place.

He didn't understand. *How...* She'd never looked more stunning to him. The blue and silver coloring of her gown enhanced her natural beauty and took his breath away. Lulia had always been exquisite to him, but he never imagined that she could be more so. He had to go to her.

He was walking toward her before he even realized his feet had started moving. They met in the middle of the room, and it seemed as if no one else existed. She wore an exquisite gown that did wonderful things to her décolletage.

"Hello," she said. Her voice had a demureness to it that hadn't been there before.

"You're as lovely as ever," he complimented her. "Lady Lulia Vasile Alby." He lifted a brow. "Are you keeping secrets from me?"

"Not intentionally," she answered. "Or perhaps a little bit. It's not something many are aware of. My grandfather was the Earl of Chaucerton. Diana is my cousin."

"Yes," he said more to himself than her. "You mentioned that you considered her family, but she really is a relation of yours."

She nodded. "Our grandfather didn't want anyone to realize my connection to the family. He was embarrassed by my gypsy roots—the earl disowned my father when he married my mother. When they died, he threatened me, so I stopped using the Alby name. I thought my entire family would disown me as well if they really knew me, so I never told Diana of our connection. At least not until a couple days ago... It was time."

"I see," he replied and glanced away from her. "When were you going to tell me?"

"I'm not certain..." He met her gaze. She nibbled on her lips and appeared a little nervous. "Diana decided for me tonight. She wants everyone to know we are family. She refuses to let the Earl of Chaucerton's previous edict dictate anything to her. She doesn't much like our grandfather, and besides she is Lady Northesk now. Her marriage gives her an untouchable aura."

"What about you?" She didn't have the protection of marriage. Her grandfather could and might decide she needed to be punished for her actions. Fin didn't want anything to happen to her. He... loved her. "Who's going to ensure you're all right?"

She shrugged. "I'll be fine. You needn't worry about me. I've taken care of myself this long, and I'll continue to do so."

But he didn't want her to have to go through life alone. Fin wanted to be by her side through it all.

She had become important to him. No, she'd always been essential. It had taken him a while to figure it out. "Sometimes a person meets their destiny on the very road they were on to avoid it." Fin brushed his hand over her hair. "I ran away from you and the pain of my father's death. It seemed like the only choice I had at the time. I evaded it all, and still I somehow found where I always belonged when I wasn't paying attention."

Her lips tilted upward into a warm smile. "You selected which path to take without consciously realizing it."

"Yes," he agreed. "I chose you." Fin wanted to kiss her the way he had at Vauxhall Gardens, but it wouldn't be wise in the middle of the ballroom. "May I have the pleasure of the first waltz?"

She grinned. "You can have the pleasure of all the dances on my card. I didn't bother to bring one. There's only one gentleman I wish to lead me onto the floor."

When he'd agree to attend the soiree with the Duke of Ashley, he never thought he'd realize how much he loved her. He should not have run away from her all those years ago. Maybe they could have had more time together if he hadn't. He couldn't go back and change that mistake, but he could do something that would ensure their future. "Will you marry me?"

She jerked backward, as if startled by the question. "You're not asking because you want to protect me from my evil grandfather, are you?"

"No," he answered. "Though I must admit that would be an additional advantage. As my duchess, he wouldn't dare try to hurt you, and probably would try to mend the rift in your relationship."

Lulia scrunched her nose up. "I have no desire for that."

He didn't really blame her. Fin wouldn't want to become more acquainted with a man who'd made him miserable either. "Are you going to make me ask again?"

Lulia blew out a breath. "Marrying you is the one thing I wanted and never thought I had a right to wish for. So yes, I'll be happy to become your wife and spend the rest of my days by your side."

"I can get a special license, and we can marry before we travel back to Tenby as we planned to do." He lifted her hand caressed her palm with the pad of his thumb. "I know it's not much of a wedding trip, but as long as you're by my side, I'll have everything." Lulia would always be the love of his life. "We should find some place quiet." He had no idea where they could have a moment of peace in the Montford house.

"Pardon me," a young blonde woman interrupted them. "I couldn't help overhearing..."

Lulia lifted a brow. "It's rude to listen to someone else's conversation."

"Then you shouldn't have it in a crowded ballroom where anyone can hear it," the lady chastised her. "I am Lady Helena, and this is my home."

Fin's lips twitched a little bit as she introduced herself. She was lovely, but he preferred Lulia's dark hair to Lady Helena's blonde tresses. "It's a pleasure to meet you. Did you need something from us?"

"No," she answered. "But it's Christmas, and I'm feeling—generous. You wish to be alone, and I can give you that gift."

He didn't know what he'd done to deserve everything being bestowed upon him, but he would send up a round of thanks at the next opportunity. "That would be wonderful."

Lady Helena's lips tilted upward. "I'm happy to see two people in love and willing to take a leap of faith. Also, I'd like an invitation to your wedding—I adore a good ceremony."

She led them out of the ballroom and to a conservatory at the back of the house. Several different types of vegetation were in full bloom. It was a lovely place for a private interlude. "I'll leave you two alone," Lady Helena said and exited the room.

Now that Lady Helena was gone they could get back to more important things. "I've wanted to kiss from the moment you arrived." Fin pulled her into his arms. "I can't wait until we can be married and we're able to begin our life together."

"Why wait? There is nothing preventing us from having the life we've always wanted." She flashed him a sultry smile. "Kiss me, Fin."

He did as she demanded and kissed Lulia with all the passion stored up inside of him. Christmastide used to be the worst time of the year for him, but now he'd have this kiss to remember for all time with the gypsy he loved...

EPILOGUE

One week later...

Fin flipped open the *London Times* preparing to read it before breakfast. He wanted to check the society pages to see if the announcement of his wedding had been reported. Normally, he didn't bother with such things, but for Lulia he would ensure proper etiquette was observed. He wanted everything to be as normal as possible. He'd obtained a marriage license immediately and married Lulia. Waiting to start their lives together hadn't sat well with him. He'd already wasted too much time already.

"Fin, Darling," she said. Her voice was sweet and alluring. He glanced over the edge of the paper immediately forgetting what he'd been about to do.

"Yes?" He lifted a brow. "What is it?"

"Have you read the latest in Whispers from Lady X?"

He pushed his nose up in confusion, and then, he recalled Dashville rambling about a Lady X during their gathering at White's. "Isn't that the scandal matron everyone hates?" He was presuming that last bit. The marquess certainly didn't like him much. Fin didn't see why anyone would deign to like her.

"Oh, yes," Lulia answered. "She's the best. I've always wondered how she manages to gather her gossip. It seems as if she knows everyone..."

"What do you find so intriguing in this particular column?" He set the Times down on the table. "I admit I've never read her sheet."

Lulia gasped and set the scandal paper down. "Fin..." She opened her mouth and then shut it. Little giggles erupted from her gorgeous lips. "I should have known you wouldn't bother with the latest gossip. You don't suffer fools and don't bother with anything as unimportant as idle musings, but you should read this." She slid the paper over to him. He picked it up and perused the infamous lady of whispers words.

My dear readers...

It is my pleasure to announce the nuptials of the Duke of Clare and Lady Lulia Vasile Alby. I would have reported their romance sooner, but I decided to respect their privacy over the holiday season. Even I enjoy a good romantic story every now and then, and trust me, theirs is one for the ages. Sometimes you find love when you're not looking for it, and sometimes, it's always been there. I've never witnessed two people more suited to each other than His Grace and Miss Vasile Alby. My apologies...it's Her Grace now. May you have a wonderful life together and enjoy being the biggest scandal of the year, or rather, the end of it. You're sure to give me a lot of material over the coming months, and for that, I'm eternally grateful.

--Lady X

Fin set the sheet down and shook his head. There were not a lot of individuals privy to the details of their wedding. The announcement was scheduled to be in the *Times* today. How could Lady X have uncovered the information already? They only married a few days ago... "How often do you read this?"

"I've never missed an issue," she responded. "Why?"

"Has Lady X ever mentioned me before?" He didn't know why he was suddenly curious, but he couldn't help asking. As often as Dashville said he appeared… What if she discussed Fin and his inability to socialize? How mortifying that would be.

"She'd never mentioned you before." Lulia tilted her head to the side. "I've been mentioned as that scandalous gypsy several times, but never by name. Actually, her favorite subject is the Marquess of Dashville. I don't know what he did to incur her wrath, but I'm glad she doesn't hate me as she does him."

He nodded and mumbled, "Quite agree." Maybe Dashville had a reason to hate the gossip queen. "Dashville has complained about her. I guess I didn't realize he wasn't being dramatic about it."

Lulia laughed. "I'll see if I have any of the previous sheets for you to read. I pity Dashville. Lady X definitely wants to see him ruined." She shrugged. "I have to admit it is nice to see that she's written something pleasant about us. She can be kind when it is warranted."

"Are you happy?" Fin couldn't help asking. He didn't like that Lulia was ever mistreated. "I know that we've not been married long…" All he wanted was for her to have everything her heart desired. Was that too much to ask?

"I am, but you needn't worry over me. There's

nothing I could want more than to spend the rest of my life with you. I never believed I'd be a wife or that I'd have love. It was something other people found, not me. So to have this with you and to have a future full of surprises waiting for us—there's nothing more I could ever ask for."

He reached over and pulled her into his lap. She pressed her lips to his and warmth spread through him. Lulia brought out the best in him and he was lucky she loved him. Fin made a vow to never take her or life for granted. Lady X was right about one thing—love had always been there between them. Now that they realized it they had a future he didn't dream he could ever have. Life happens while you're making other plans, and he was grateful that love had found its way to him.

EXCERPT: ODDS OF LOVE

SCANDAL MEETS LOVE 4

Dawn Brower

PROLOGUE

January 1816

Snow trickled down from the sky and blanketed the ground. Lady Katherine Wilson pulled her cloak tighter around her and did her best to suppress a shiver. The frigid temperature managed to seep underneath the wool cloak and spread over her. She wanted desperately to reach her destination and escape from the cold. She hated winter. It had never been her favorite time of year, and today was no different. It would be better if she could stay home and sit in front of the fire in the sitting room. Even Fortuna's Parlor would be preferable. To be fair each day since her grandmother passed away had been dismal though. What she didn't want to do was visit with solicitors and discuss her loss in depth. Her grandmother was gone. Hadn't she suffered enough already?

She finally reached the offices of her grandmother's solicitor and stepped up to the doorway, and knocked. Katherine had never been to a solicitor before and had no clue what to do. What exactly was the proper protocol when dealing with a solicitor? The finishing school she'd attended hadn't prepared her for this particular circumstance. She probably could have asked Narissa or even Diana, but she hadn't wanted to burden them with her troubles.

The door opened and an older gentleman filled the entryway. He had dark hair with salt and pepper strands streaked through the sides. His dark waistcoat gave him a somber appearance that reflected in his ice blue eyes. Something about him seemed familiar but Katherine couldn't place him in her memory. "Lady Katherine," he greeted her. "Please come in out of the cold."

Had she met him previously? How had he known her at a glance? She would have to inquire during their meeting. "Mr. Adamson?" Katherine lifted a brow. She wanted to make sure he was the solicitor she had to a meeting with.

"Yes," he answered as he gestured her past the doorway and closed it behind her.

Katherine shivered. The cold hadn't quite left her even with the warmth that already enveloped her. Sadly, after the conference she'd have to walk home in the awful weather. She really wished a carriage had been available to her, but her mother had used it to pay calls.

"Can I take your cloak?" Mr. Adamson asked.

She wanted to keep it on because she was still a little cold; however, soon it would be too warm and it was better to take it off now. Besides she wasn't sure how long their conversation would take. Katherine shrugged the cloak off and handed it to him. He placed it on a nearby hook and then turned toward her. "Follow me. You'll be more comfortable in the office. There's a fire in the hearth and its much warmer."

Mr. Adamson led her to the office and gestured toward a chair. He sat behind a desk and shuffled some papers before glancing back at her. "You're probably wondering why I asked you to meet me here. Normally I'd conduct a visit such as this one in the comfort of the client's home. But because of the nature of your grandmother's last wishes I'm required to do it here. She was afraid that if we met at your father's home he'd try to take control of the assets she left to you. Not that he could have..." He cleared his throat and then continued, "But this makes things simpler for you. There is no conflict to deal with and once you leave you will have control of your inheritance."

What could her grandmother have left for her? She thought her father had inherited all of her grandmother's possessions. Not that Katherine expected her to have much. Most of the estate had already gone to her father when his father passed. It was part of the entailment. Her grandmother lived in a house in Sussex county, near Heathfield. She had always assumed it was the dower house though... "I am not certain I understand."

He handed her a letter. "It is all explained here. You're a very wealthy young lady."

Katherine took the missive from him and broke the seal. "It's from my grandmother..." She recognized her handwriting immediately. Her heart beat heavily in her chest and she fought the urge to cry. She'd been letting her sadness get the best o her for longer than she would have liked. Katherine missed her grandmother terribly.

"Keep reading," Mr. Adamson encouraged her. "It's important you read it until the end."

Katherine turned her attention back to her grandmother's words. What could she have had to say that she couldn't say before she passed away?

My Dearest Grandchild,

Your heart must be heavy, and I'm sorry for the pain you are now feeling. If I could take all your hurt away I would, but if you're reading this then I must no longer be with you. My death, while painful, gives you freedom in ways you probably never imagined. My son, your father, is a harsh man and has not given you the love you need. He learned his behaviors from his own father. My marriage was an arranged one and my mother made assurances that I'd always be provided for. In England, property is immediately owned by a woman's husband after marriage vows are said. My mother didn't believe a woman should be controlled by a man. Love isn't the main requirement in marriage and often doesn't play a part in the contract settlements. That was the case with my own nuptials. A Dukedom such as Gladstone was forged on the bonds of many unions. John was destitute and agreed to all the contractual stipulations before I married him. It was never my desire to become a duchess, but it made my father practically salivate, but I digress.

The important thing you need to understand is

that I was never a pawn, and you don't need to be either. My money was controlled by me, but a generous sum was bestowed upon John after we said our vows. He had his money, and I had mine. I provided him with his heir and after that we lived separate lives. Luckily, John didn't waste his money and rebuilt the Gladstone estates. Charles is more his son than mine. Don't let him control you. Seize control of your life.

There are so many things I want to say to you, but the most important last words I can leave you with is this. Marry for love and nothing more. My estate is yours. Use it wisely, my dear. I trust you will make the right decisions. You have the ability to choose your own path now. Happiness can be yours, and love as well.

All my love,

Grandmother

Katherine wiped a tear from her cheek. Her father wasn't always hard, but she understood what her grandmother meant. Her father wanted to control everything and everyone around him. He hated to be thwarted.

Katherine glanced at Mr. Adamson and asked, "What exactly did my grandmother leave me?"

"As the letter states—her entire estate," he responded matter-of-factly.

"I understand, but what does her estate entail?" She repressed the urge to roll her eyes. "She says I'm wealthy now. Does she mean I have unlimited funds?"

"You do have a sizeable bank account now. There is approximately ten thousand pounds in her account," he answered. "She also left you a horse farm in Sussex. That was your grandmother's main estate and she had a cottage near Bath that you now own. The farm brings in around five thousand pounds per annum"

Katherine's mouth fell open. That was a lot of money... She could do anything she wanted just as her grandmother said in her letter, but Katherine hadn't fully appreciated her words until she heard what she'd inherited. "And my father can't take it away from me?" It was a concern because her father didn't like anyone having more than he did. She couldn't say the state of the dukedom, but that amount of money would surely rival it. He would want it and control of the farm.

"No," he said. "The contracts were clear. Any money she had could only be given to a direct female relation of hers. The only way your father would have inherited it would have been if there were no females to inherit." He lifted his lips upward. "Even then, the first female born of her direct bloodline would gain control of the assets. A male can only retain guardianship of it until a female is born. It's a matriarchal estate."

There were so many possibilities available to her. She wasn't sure what she should do first. Never in her wildest dreams would she have foreseen this happening. Her grandmother's death was the worst and best thing that had ever happened to her. Why hadn't she told her that she'd inherit so much from her? Did she think it would have made a difference in their relationship? Her grandmother had always meant so much to her.

"Is there anything I need to do?" Katherine's mind was still reeling from the news. "Can I go to the farm?"

Her grandmother had always visited her. She'd never been to her estate in Sussex. Katherine had a sudden desire to be amongst her things and the place she loved. It might help her feel closer to her grandmother again. It might be silly, but she needed it.

"There is nothing required of you. Everything has been put into your name. There's nothing you need to do but accept your inheritance. If you require anything please let me know and I'll see to it." He slid a stack of papers toward her. "These are for your records. I keep a copy here if they're ever lost and yes, to answer your question, you may visit the farm. If you so desire, you may relocate to Sussex permanently. There's no reason for you to remain at the ducal estate or under your father's care."

That settled it for her. She would go home and pack, then set off for the farm in Sussex. Traveling in winter wasn't her favorite, but to be away from her father would be a blessing. She didn't tell even her closest friends how horrible he could be. Diana and Narissa had no idea how hard it could be for her to sneak out of the house or even to openly gain permission to attend a function. She didn't live the happy-go-lucky life they believed she did. The main reason she'd been looking for a husband was to escape her father's control. Now she didn't have to marry unless she wanted to. She was free to live her life and not worry about anything ever again.

"Thank you so much." Katherine came to her feet. "How soon can I travel there?"

"I can have a carriage ready to take you at any time. When do you wish to go?" He stood and walked around the desk to her side. "The servants already are aware of your ownership and expect you to visit. They're anxious to meet you. They all loved your grandmother."

"I'd like to go at first light tomorrow." Katherine couldn't wait to meet the servants. If they loved her grandmother as she did they'd have much to discuss. "Is that too soon?"

"Not at all," he reassured her. "I'll have a carriage readied. Do you require a chaperone or are you taking your maid with you."

Betty would love to accompany her. She was the only servant in her father's household solely loyal to Katherine. "My maid will be with me." They exited his office and Mr. Adamson retrieved her cloak, then assisted her with it.

"Very well then." He smiled down at her. Where he'd seemed cold to her before he now seemed— almost fatherly, or at least how she imagined a father should be. "Don't forget to let me know if you require anything of me. Safe travels on your journey. I believe you will be pleasantly surprised by the farm. It's a wonderful place. I've visited there often on business for your grandmother."

She'd already thanked him, but it didn't seem like enough. He'd changed her life in the span of less than an hour. Yes, it really was her grandmother that had made her life more bearable, but Mr. Adamson was bearer of that bright news. "I'm sure I'll be fine; however, if something does arise I'll be sure to inform you. Have a good day." Katherine nodded to him and then exited the solicitor's office. For the first time in weeks she walked home with a smile, and not once, even in thought, did she grumble about the cold.

EXCERPT: REBELLIOUS ANGEL

CHRISTMAS WISHES 6

Dawn Brower

Dawn Brower

Rebellious
ANGEL

❄

Christmas Wishes

CHAPTER 1

September 1906

The heat wave that rocked through the country had become unbearable. For Miss Angeline Marsden it heightened her anxiety levels. She had plans her parents wouldn't appreciate, but they would, in fact, give her hell about them. A girl had to stick to her beliefs, and Angeline had many. Some battles had to be fought the hard way, and others required a little more deviousness to come out the victor. Her parent's dislike of her cause required the latter.

If she had any chance of participating in the upcoming parade, she'd need help from someone close to her. More specifically, her best friend, Lady Emilia St. John, and Angeline prayed she'd assist her. Otherwise, she didn't know how she'd manage to fool her parents. It had to work. This meant a lot to her, and she'd do just about anything to ensure it went her way.

Angeline rushed down the street toward the Huntly townhouse. Emilia was expecting her for afternoon tea. Hopefully Emilia's mother, the Duchess of Huntly, wouldn't be in residence. It might prove to be difficult to gain Emilia's assistance if they had to discuss it in whispers behind their silk fans. When she reached the door, she rapped on the knocker twice. A man with dark hair graying at the sides, opened it and greeted her, "Good day, Miss Angeline."

"Hello, Simmons." She nodded toward the aging butler. "Is Emilia in the sitting room?"

"Indeed, she is," he confirmed. "Her grace is as well."

Drat. She had hoped Emilia's mother would be out making calls instead. Normally, she'd love to visit with them both. She considered the duchess family of sorts. Her parents were close to Emilia's, and they'd grown up together. There were not many family gatherings that didn't include the Marsdens and the St. Johns. Unfortunately, though, her honorary Aunt Rubina wouldn't be any happier with Angeline's plans than her parents were. Somehow, she'd find a work-around. "Thanks, Simmons." She nodded at him. "I can find my own way there."

She didn't wait for the butler to respond. Huntly Manor had been a second home to her. Angeline was as acquainted with it as she was with the Marsden family estate. She went down the hallway and took a sharp right to enter the sitting room. It had been redecorated in dark blues and gold. The duchess had wanted a change, and the new color scheme gave the room a more elegant ambiance. A tea cart had already been delivered, and several cakes were displayed on a nearby table.

"Good afternoon," she greeted them.

The duchess wore a dark green walking dress decorated with gold buttons up the front. Her kid skin gloves matched it to perfection. She must have decided a hat was too much and had left her blonde hair unadorned. "Angeline," she said cheerfully. "It's so good of you to join us."

She smiled at the duchess. "It's been too long since we've seen each other." She leaned down and kissed her cheek. "How have you been?"

The duchess waved her hand. "You don't want to hear about our trip to the country. Noah had some estate business to handle, and I admit it was nice to rusticate at Huntly Castle. It's drafty and cooler then it is here. Can you believe this heat?"

Emilia rolled her eyes while her mother wasn't looking. The duchess would have chastised her for the unladylike behavior. Angeline repressed a laugh so she wouldn't get her friend in trouble. Emilia was a younger version of the duchess, down to the silver-gray eyes. She had even donned a similar shade of green as her mother—at times it could be disconcerting how alike they were. "Come sit." Emilia patted the cushion next to her. "Tell me what you're scheming these days."

Angeline stuck her tongue out. "I'm doing no such thing." Her friend knew her too well. There had to be a way to distract the duchess so she could find some time alone with Emilia. If she couldn't gain her assistance, her plan would be doomed. "I merely wished to visit my closest friend."

"That's lovely of you," the duchess said earnestly. "How are your mother and father?"

Hell bent on ruining my life... All right, the duchess wouldn't want to hear that from her—even if it was true. "They're both wonderful. Father was discussing the possibility of returning to the country estate. London really has become unbearable this past month. The heat is torturous." To prove that point, she flipped open her silk fan and started to wave it over her face.

"It's been a hard year for your family." Her voice held a hint of sadness to it. "With your grandfather..."

Angeline almost finished that sentence for her, but instead swallowed the lump in her throat. Her grandfather had passed away suddenly a year ago. Something that had hit her father hard—no one had ever expected the old man to die. Somehow, he had seemed so infallible. With her grandfather's unexpected passing, Angeline's father had become the next Viscount Torrington. A title he'd have gladly waited forever to claim if it had kept his father alive longer.

It was no secret that the former viscount had lived the life of a pirate before he'd married Angeline's grandmother. That had given him a dangerous aura that made any suitor interested in Angeline shake in fear. It didn't help that her own father could make a man freeze in place with one glance. Between the two men, she'd failed in securing a husband after several seasons. It was a good thing she didn't actually want a husband.

Well, that wasn't true either.

There was one man she wanted to marry, and

unfortunately, he never paid any attention to her. But that was a problem she'd consider much later— maybe never. She would not let those old wounds dictate every decision she made. There were more pressing matters she had to focus on. Winning the heart of a clueless man was the least of her worries. "Grandfather will be missed," she reassured the duchess. "He'll never be forgotten. Thor was a stubborn, arrogant bastard, but we loved him—probably a little for those traits alone."

"That he did," a male said as he walked into the room.

Angeline's heart thumped inside her chest. She closed her eyes and took a deep breath, trying to calm the rapid thrusts of the traitorous organ. All he had to do was say one word and she wanted him. It had always been that way, and no matter what she did, it didn't change. Lucian St. John, the Marquess of Severn and heir to the Huntly dukedom and not to mention, he was also her closest friends' older brother and the one man she loved beyond reason.

His dark hair and chiseled cheekbones gave him a sinfully gorgeous face, but his silver eyes spoke of a devilishness she could only guess at. He had always been a perfect gentleman with her, but she knew he had a wicked side. Not personally... No, she'd never been so lucky as to taste passion of any sort. Rumors spread in abundance of how roguish he was, and she'd always been green with envy. She wanted him to look at her and desire her the same way she'd always longed for him.

"Hello, Mother," he said and leaned down to kiss the duchess's cheek. "I hope I'm not interrupting."

"Not at all dear," the duchess replied. "Are you here to join us for tea?"

"I wish I could," he replied smoothly. "I'm here to see Father, but I wanted to come say hello before we secluded ourselves in his office."

"Estate business?" His mother lifted questioning brow. "Never mind. I'm sure he'll tell me later. Are you sure you can't visit with us a little longer?"

As much as Angeline loved studying the man who held her heart without him noticing, she had other things on her mind. If Lucian stayed, that would make her goal even more difficult to achieve. Besides, it was slowly killing her to be around him. Nothing brought out the doldrums quite like his continued oblivion. She might as well be invisible when Lucian was around. He didn't bother to greet her unless good manners dictated he acknowledge her presence. Even now, he didn't turn his head and say the simplest of hellos to her or Emilia. He kept his attention focused on his mother.

"I must decline." His voice even appeared to hold a tinge of disappointment. Angeline doubted Lucian held an ounce of regret inside of him. Sure, he loved his mother, but he'd been decreed the wickedest of rogues. He probably would rather spend time in the company of a more delectable sort of female. Lucian was nothing if not smooth. "Perhaps we can have a family dinner later this week." Angeline swallowed the distaste in her mouth. Why had she gone and fallen in love with him? He'd never love her in return...

The duchess smiled, happiness radiating from her. "What a lovely idea." She turned to Emilia. "You can help me plan it, dear." Then she glanced back at Lucian. "We'll send a note to your townhouse when we decide upon a date. Go meet with your father. You know how he hates to be kept waiting."

"You're right," Lucian agreed. "Enjoy your tea." With those words, he left them alone in the sitting room.

Angeline couldn't help staring at him as he exited. Her gaze seemed to naturally follow after him whenever he was in the immediate vicinity. Would she ever put her feelings for him behind her? She held back a sigh. It wouldn't help further her cause—any of them.

"Emilia," Angeline turned toward her. "It's such a lovely day. Do you care to go for a stroll with me?"

"Have you gone mad?" Emilia crinkled her eyebrows together. "It's as hot as the dickens outside." She flipped open her silk fan and waved it furiously over her flushed face. "I'd rather not exert myself any more than necessary."

This time Angeline did sigh. Emilia had a valid point, but she was running out of options. She wanted her help, so she'd have to figure out another way of discussing her problem with Emilia privately. "I'm...restless. I thought walking would help."

"Didn't you walk here, dear?" the duchess asked, her tone held a hint of skepticism to it. "I'd have thought that was more than enough exercise."

Her home wasn't far from Huntly Manor, so she didn't see any reason to have a carriage hitched for the short distance—even on a sweltering day. "If Emilia doesn't want to join me, that's her decision." Angeline had to hold back from reaching over and shaking her friend. She'd have to wait until the Wharton dinner later to find some alone time with her. "Perhaps I should skip tea and make my way home."

Her afternoon call hadn't gone as planned. She'd also had to suffer through time spent in Lucian's company—not that he'd acknowledged her. Maybe that was part of her problem. She'd longed for him since she was ten and two. Nine years later and her heart still skipped a beat whenever he neared.

"I didn't mean to imply you're not welcome," the duchess said. "Please don't feel as if you have to leave."

Angeline stood and went to the duchess to pull her into a hug. "You're gracious as always Aunt Ruby —it is as I said. I'm restless." She didn't want to make the duchess feel that she'd done anything wrong. It couldn't be further from the truth. If anyone could be held accountable for her agitation, it would be Lucian. She'd been on edge before she arrived at Huntly Manor, but his proximity made it even worse. Angeline stepped back. "Don't worry everything is fine, and I'll see you tonight at the Wharton dinner."

Emilia stood and wound her arm with Angeline's. "I'll see you out if you're so insistent on leaving before you've had any tea."

She scrunched up her nose. "It is hot out, and

while I am parched, tea seems—too much right now."
Truthfully, she'd lost her appetite—if she ever had
one—the moment Lucian had stepped into the sitting
room.

"It's never too hot for tea," Emilia replied. "Perhaps there's something else bothering you?" The
corner of her mouth tilted upward into a sly smile.
Her friend knew her to well...

They exited the room and walked down the hall
leading to the foyer. Angeline didn't bother to
comment on Emilia's not-so-subtle hint at Lucian's
presence interrupting tea. "We'll have to talk more
later. There's something I want to discuss with you."

"About Lucian?"

Angeline rolled her eyes. "Of course not. He's..."
Drat. In a perfect world, he'd be her everything. Too
bad Lucian would never reciprocate. "As much as I
long for him to love me, he never will. You more than
anyone know that. This is something more
important."

"My brother is a fool," Emilia said and placed
her hand on Angeline's. "We will talk more at the
dinner. I'll help you with anything."

Emilia had always been there for her. Hopefully
she was still willing to help once she realized what
Angeline needed. She hugged her friend and left the

manor. She had a lot to consider before the dinner later that night. Lucian could go to hell. He was probably the ruler of that fiery pit and the reason they were inundated with the unseasonably warm weather.

All right, he wasn't *that* bad... She wished he loved her though. However, no amount of hoping for the impossible would make it true.

EXCERPT: STEALING A ROGUE'S KISS

Amanda Mariel

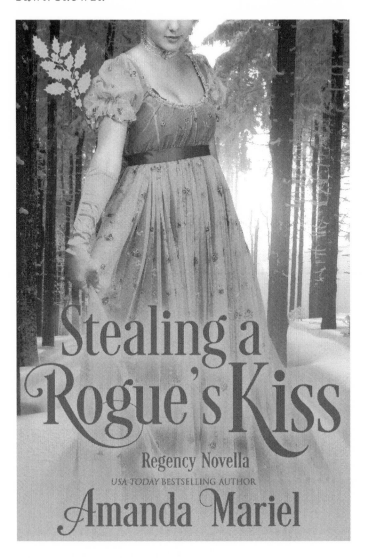

Stealing a
Rogue's Kiss

Regency Novella

USA TODAY BESTSELLING AUTHOR

Amanda Mariel

CHAPTER 1

London, England

ONE, *two, three, four...*Lady Daphne Rosamond counted her steps as she paced the length of the lady's retiring room at the Hawthorn ball. She should be in the ballroom. Gentlemen should be paying her attention. She should be dancing and flirting. Three seasons, for three long tedious seasons Daphne had sat on the sidelines hoping and praying that some worthy gentleman would take notice.

"There you are. I've been searching for you." Daphne's cousin, Lady Natalie St. Vela strolled into the room with Miss Lulia Vasile at her side. Natalie paused, drawing her brows together as she studied Daphne. "Is something the matter?"

"No...yes...I don't know," Daphne stuttered, attempting to collect her thoughts.

Natalie narrowed her gaze.

Daphne's cheeks warmed under her cousin's scrutiny. "I've grown weary of sitting on the sidelines. Perhaps it is time I accept my fate and give in to being an old maid."

Lulia drew closer, her violet eyes skeptical. "How do you know such a fate awaits you?"

Daphne waved her hands over her body. "Look at me. I'm plump and shy; not at all the type of woman that gentlemen take notice of. In my three seasons, I've only danced a handful of times. No-one has ever come to call, let alone court me."

"Oh Daphne," Natalie rested a hand on her shoulder, "you are lovely. Any gentleman would be lucky to have you. Do not be so hard on yourself."

Daphne closed her eyes fighting back tears. How she wished Natalie's words were true, but they unequivocally were not. Daphne possessed and a kind and reserved nature, but she lacked all of the other qualities a man looked for in a wife. She'd never be an English beauty, nor would she ever be comfortable in a crowded room. She shook her head. "You're wrong."

"Take off your glove." Lulia notched her chin. "Let me have a look at your palm."

Daphne swallowed as she stared at the woman, confusion muddling her thoughts. "My glove?"

Lulia nodded, her raven curls bouncing. "Yes, your glove."

Natalie reached for Daphne's hand then began unbuttoning the white satin glove that covered it. "Lulia reads palms. Let her have a look and she will tell you what your future holds."

Daphne jerked back her hand, her gaze flittering from one woman to the next. She did not believe in such nonsense. Fortunetellers were nothing more than frauds—that's what mama had always told her.

"What have you got to lose?" Natalie reached for her hand again.

Daphne interlocked her finger's stopping the assault. "Mama says—"

"Blah, blah," Natalie interrupted. "Stop stalling and remove your glove."

Lulia smiled, her eyes sparkling. "Your mama says that fortune tellers are frauds. She's right you know."

Daphne stared at her in shock. How could she

admit to such at the very same time she was attempting to read Daphne's future?

"Most of them are, but a well-trained gypsy hones her craft. I spent years working on mine." Lulia flipped her hand over and began tracing the lines of her palm. "This one is my lifeline. This is my love line. Our hands reveal much about our fates."

A spark of hope swelled in Daphne's chest. Perhaps Lulia did possess a true talent. Maybe she really could tell Daphne's fortune. If so, wouldn't she wish to hear it? Daphne fumbled with her glove, pulling her hand free of the satin confines.

Lulia took Daphne's hand in hers and began studying the lines. She trailed her fingertip across one, down another. Daphne tried to relax, but her heart beat fiercely as she watched. What if Lulia only told her what she wished to hear? What if she confirmed her fears? Either way, Daphne feared what would be said. She pulled her hand free. "This is a mistake. I don't want to know."

"Nonsense." Natalie shook her head. "You're just afraid of what Lulia will find. Get your head out of the sand and take control of your life."

Daphne's blood warmed, anger sweeping through her at Natalie's harsh words. "You have no idea what you speak of. I beg you to keep your opinions to yourself." Daphne snatched her glove from Natalie and tugged it back on.

How unlike her to act is such a brash manner. She never raised her voice. Never grew so angry that she could not cancel the emotion.

"Are you sure you do not wish to hear what I have to convey?" Lulia asked.

Daphne hesitated, her mind swirling with uncertainty. Part of her desperately wished to hear what Lulia saw; the rest of her feared the outcome. Natalie had been correct; Daphne was a coward.

"Of course she wants to know," Natalie said.

Lulia gave a gentle smile. "Daphne?"

Daphne drew in a slow breath, exhaling it even slower. "Yes. Tell me."

You are not destined to be alone. Love may enter your life, true love. The deeply seeded kind that inspires poems and endures for all time." She recaptured Daphne's hand then peeled her glove off. "See this?" She trailed her fingertip over the line below Daphne's pinky.

Daphne nodded, tears pricking her eyes once more. The hope welling within her was nearly too much for her to handle.

"This is your love line. It's straight and long indicating a deep and long love."

Natalie rested one hand on her hip, cocking it slightly as a smug grin spread over her face. "See, Daphne, I told you there was nothing to fear. You need only get out of your own way. Stop hiding in corners and welcome love to find you."

Daphne could not argue for she'd long been a wallflower. Her cousin understood her well and knew her even better. All the same, Daphne would never be comfortable in crowds the way that Natalie was. She simply wasn't the outgoing social butterfly that her cousin was.

Lulia gave a gentle squeeze to Daphne's hand before releasing it. "I'm afraid your situation is not as simple as all that. Love will not just land in your lap."

Daphne pulled her lower lip in, nibbling on it. This entire conversation was lunacy. She should not be engaging in any of it. Mama would not approve, and the emotional toll on Daphne was quickly proving too much.

"Your time is coming to an end. If you do not receive a kiss by Christmastide, you will continue through life unwed."

"Christmastide?" Daphne's hands shook, her heart crumbling as any hope she'd had fled. "That is impossible. It's but a fortnight away and I haven't a single admirer. Worse, I will be leaving for the country on the marrow."

Natalie took her elbow and leaned closer. "Stop being so dramatic. It's not at all like you to behave in such a way."

"You're right and I'm sorry, but you know I speak the truth." Daphne would be spending the holiday at Natalie's family home, Harington Gardens. Her uncle, the Duke of Sheridan insisted the entire family grace him with their presence, and her mama and papa had readily agreed.

Not that Daphne minded, she enjoyed spending time at the sprawling estate as well as with Natalie, but finding a suitor would prove impossible. She couldn't very well go around the village hoping for random strangers to kiss her and the estate would be full of her relations. It was hopeless.

"You are giving up before you even begin." Natalie wrapped an arm around Daphne pulling her close. "But all is not lost, you'll see."

Lulia gave a sympathetic grin. "Trust in your future and make things happen. You'll be glad you did."

Daphne nodded, portraying a confidence she most defiantly did not feel. She feared the only thing any of them would be seeing was her fast becoming an old maid. All the same, she would embrace the bit of hope Lulia had bestowed on her as well as Natalie's encouragement and hope for something more.

One fortnight, fourteen days…Soon she would know her future.

ABOUT THE AUTHOR

USA TODAY Bestselling author, DAWN BROWER writes both historical and contemporary romance. There are always stories inside her head; she just never thought she could make them come to life. That creativity has finally found an outlet.

Growing up she was the only girl out of six children. She is a single mother of two teenage boys; there is never a dull moment in her life. Reading books is her favorite hobby and she loves all genres.

Earl of Harrington

A Lady Hoyden's Secret

One Wicked Kiss

Earl In Trouble

All the Ladies Love Coventry

Marsden Descendants

Rebellious Angel

Tempting An American Princess

Marsden Romances

A Flawed Jewel

A Crystal Angel

A Treasured Lily

A Sanguine Gem

A Hidden Ruby

A Discarded Pearl

Novak Springs

Cowgirl Fever

Dirty Proof

Unbridled Pursuit

Sensual Games

Christmas Temptation

The Magical Hunt

Ever Beloved

Forever My Earl

Always My Viscount

Infinitely My Marquess